NUMAN VERSUS NUMAN

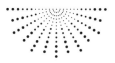

NICKY BLUE

START HERE

Hi, Thanks for buying my book. Make yourself comfortable and let's get cracking. I do normally try to get around to everyone with soft drinks and light snacks, but my sciatica has been giving me a bit of gyp lately. So, don't hold your breath.

If you would like to see some of the Numan Versus Numan promo video outtakes, and get some of my books for free. Join my readers list here:

www.nickyblue.com/reads

Dear Gary

I had this thing happen.
I can't seem to shut it out.
Every time I close my eyes it's there waiting for me.
It feels like it's getting worse.
Tina thinks I'm being pathetic.
She's the one person that should understand.
Thanks for listening, Gary.
I can't talk about it with anyone else.
I know I can trust you.

Five

TWISTED WING

23rd October, 11.30a.m.

C lear skies had been somewhat of a rare commodity of late. Taking off from the brow of Cabin Hill, Five felt like a golden eagle, soaring and untainted, glorious and unfettered. The brave kingdom of the Saxons stretched out before him, its ghost warriors flew beside him reminding him of the civilisations that have risen and fallen on these ripped up patchwork fields. A thermal lifted him high into a lapis sky – immeasurable beauty. *If only I could keep this feeling.* Pausing briefly to look down over Chigwell Water Works, he pulled down hard on the control line to follow the brook east-bound through Hainault Forest. The sycamore leaves had now turned yellow but the damp earthy scent of moss and pine still lit up his senses, even from up here. There was a majesty weaved into the soul of this woodland, it wasn't just rusty bicycle frames and used Durex. He dipped lower to hover above the tree canopy. This was once a royal hunting ground, fresh game for the king's table. There was still plenty of hunting to be had in Romford, though most of it happened in Denny's nightclub. On Saturdays they did two fights for the price of one and if you didn't pull, the manageress took you back to her place. If that particular delicacy was not to your désir du coeurs, you could have always delighted in an aperitif at the Asylum wine bar. Never so completely had a venue been encapsulated by its name. A crosswind blew him past the landing strip in Cottons Park and dangerously low over the traffic on London Road. After narrowly avoiding a phone mast he was forced to come down on the roof of the shopping centre. That wasn't meant to happen. The police were called. It's a good job the band's roadie was head of security.

'What in fuck's name are you playing at?'

'I was distracted,' said Five.

'I wish I never got you into paragliding,' said Stubber, pacing the tired parquet flooring of his top floor office. 'Do you know how much that wing cost?'

'You bought it did you?' Five arched an eyebrow.

'You know what I mean,' Stubber replied by crop dusting his head with a fine mist of saliva. 'My job's on the line 'cos of this, I'm supposed to retire next year. I've got Sheila from the fish counter running around telling everyone that Al-Qaeda are on the roof.'

'And how many times have I covered for you?' Five rubbed at the eczema in the crease of his left arm through his fake leather biker jacket.

'You on about last Saturday? If you must know, I did offer to give her a lift home but she only wanted her husband to watch through the back of the van window.'

'How romantic.'

'I'm not into any of that weird stuff.'

'I'm sure that would put Barbara's mind at rest.'

Stubber stopped in his tracks and stared Five hard in the eyes.

'We're doing blackmail now are we?'

'Let's call it friendship.'

'Go on then, piss off, I'll say you got out the window.' Stubber took a deep drag on his vaporiser and vanished into a mist of rhubarb and custard.

Not one to be rushed, Five found a toilet and redid his smudged eyeliner – even goths don't want to look like pandas. Not that he was ever strictly a goth. He had invented the term 'progressive alternative', or prog. alt. for short. It was going to be the next big thing apparently. He'd remained convinced of it for nearly twenty years. Putting foundation on when he hadn't shaved was never a good idea but that's the thing about being in a band – it's a responsibility – you were always on stage. Not that he was the archetypal walking billboard. He wore his baseball cap pulled down low over his face (he said it stopped too much reality getting in). For those familiar with his face, his eyes carried a concoction of blind hope and committed denial, infused with the terror of an impending, earth-shattering catastrophe. He would scurry past people, attempting to get by unnoticed, as if one misplaced comment could have crushed him like a snowflake. Having spooned on the requisite amount of slap, he squeezed his wing and harness into his rucksack and crept out into the corridor, clutching his helmet. He promptly headed for the fire escape, which conveniently delivered him close enough to the loading bay to scuttle out unseen. It was time to go home and attempt to catch up with his never-ending list of caring duties.

It was only 3pm but the light was fading. A damp fog had crept in to strangle the remains of the day. Since the council downgraded the brightness of the street lights, it was hard to see one foot in front of the other in such conditions. The only things that could pierce the murk were the red lights flickering intermittently from the three giant cranes that filled the skyline. They orchestrated the renovation work on the industrial park, and towered over Romford like an alien race of praying mantis, jealously guarding their prey. They dominated the view from Five's bedroom window, which is the reason he always kept his curtains closed. He couldn't bear to look at them. Pulling up the lapels of his jacket to limit the moisture from penetrating his neckline, Five wondered what he would cook everyone for dinner. When you are the sole carer for your entire family, life is all about clandestine deals and astute political manoeuvring.

When he first started the role, the arrangement was he would only cook vegan food, the prospect of cooking dead flesh being abhorrent to him. It was only his dad Frank, who refused to give up his lifelong addiction to meat and two veg, complaining with a myriad of assertions that it's what all animals do in the wild. After much soul searching Five agreed to cook two separate meals – and why not? It's good to add extra levels of complexity to an already impossible job. To avoid ethical incongruence, however, Five bought some very realistic meat-free sausages and burgers. Frank can't get enough of them. It pained Five to know that for all his dad's protests he unwittingly remained the strictest vegan in the whole of Romford. But like his wise brother Don always says, morality can be a messy business.

Setting off down Waterloo Road, he turned the corner into London Road and stopped abruptly after seeing the damp had driven the snails onto the pavements. He hated the way people walked over them, – crunching and popping their shells – without a second thought. He knelt down and began picking them up, placing them on the grassy verge. Bent double in the murky half-light, rain started to patter on the pavement next to him. *This is no job for a 56-year-old.* He knew they would be back on the pavement again as soon as he left; he was about to give it up as a bad idea when he heard footsteps approaching behind him.

'Afternoon brother!'

He looked up to see his old school mate staring down at him. Peter Hampton, affectionately known to his few remaining mates as 'Conspiracy Pete' was the other class weirdo at the local grammar school. Both aspiring towards the arts, they had formed a strong friendship based around the need for an alternative education and the Romford comprehensive school survival strategy of safety in numbers. Pete reckoned as radical liberal intelligentsia they should be reading *The Guardian* but, after a few weeks, they opted for the *Melody Maker* because it was 25 pence cheaper and full of punk girls. What was left of Pete's hair was bright green and when he was outside he always wore a disposable face mask ('You can't be too careful these days, those chemtrails will be the death of us all').

'Hey mate, what you up to?' Five clambered to his feet and, giving Pete a bear hug, a week-old application of patchouli oil assaulted his senses.

Pete winked and pointed to the taped-up laptop tucked under his arm.

'How about you?'

'Mum teamed up with the doctor to send me for one of those carers assessments, they think I'm not coping. They've made me an appointment to see a counsellor.'

'Fuck that, don't let 'em get in your head. It's the only place they can't get to us.'

'I'm only going to keep her happy.'

'Do you remember Reggie Taylor from school? He was having problems with his misses and she forced him into marriage guidance. He was the most sorted bloke you could meet, wasn't he?'

Five nodded tentatively.

'They ended up doing a lobotomy on him.'

'No way.'

'You'd get more sense out of a black bean burrito these days.'

Five attempted a change of conversation by pointing at Pete's laptop.

'Is it bust?'

Pete pulled a 360 recon. and moved in so close that Five could see the layers of encrusted gunk between his eyelashes.

'Webcam's been compromised,' Pete whispered, his eyes darting up and down the street as if they were being operated by a lever in the back of his head.'

'Someone watching you?'

'You carrying a mobile or a Nectar card?'

'Yeah?'

Just when he thought Pete couldn't get any closer, he did. He enacted a zip closing along his lips, then mouthed, 'pop round tomorrow?'

'We've got a big band meeting tomorrow, but I definitely will soon.'

With that, Pete disappeared into Cottons Park to seek out anonymity with the rats and shadows.

Alone in the murkiness, Five weighed up his quickest options for getting home. He didn't like being out after dark as he always felt like he was being followed. It wasn't something he could ever prove; his girlfriend Tina thought it proved he was paranoid. He took the decision to go down a narrow side alley behind the shops on London Road. It normally meant navigating broken bottles and snarling teenagers but it would be a lot quicker.

As he passed the backyard of the undertakers something caught his attention through the slats in the rear gate. It was the outlines of two men hovering over an open coffin. A red neon glow radiated up from the coffin, illuminating their faces. The tallest of the men wore a long leather trench coat that touched the tops of his scuffed army boots. He pointed at a packing crate across the yard.

'Get some more.'

Looking down, Five noticed a bottle of electric blue hair

colouring in a recycling box and a cold shot of recognition washed over him. He knew exactly who this was: Ross from The Storm Troopers. His nemesis. The man who had stolen his crown as the leading Gary Numan tribute artist. A crown that should still be his. *What the hell are they up to?* Five dug his nails into the crease of his arm and recoiled as a razor-sharp pain ricocheted through his body.

Ross's squat companion walked over to the crate and grabbed an armful of red neon wires and what looked like broken machine parts. He came back to the coffin and dumped them inside.

Crouching down towards the coffin, Ross turned to his companion.

'I think they're moving, get the lid on, quick.'

The guy walked towards the gate, causing Five to jerk backwards and hit a metal dustbin. Its lid flipped off and hit the ground with a sharp crash.

'What's that?'

Five quickly ducked out of view and sprinted for as fast and long as he could manage. Only when he got to the safety of the high street did he pause to cough up bile and take in the cold damp air.

Running was one of the things Five did best. Running and keeping secrets. Skills that he had been trying to hone to perfection only to find they were serving him less and less with each passing day. When he got home, his dad Frank was watching a nature program about an insect called a twisted-wing parasite. It escaped detection by disguising itself in the skin of its victim, burrowing into its body and devouring it from within. It struck Five that it was similar to having a secret you can't tell anyone. It slowly eats away at you and, however hard you try, there is nothing you can do to stop it.

2

HEARTS AND MINDS

25th October

Five dragged himself out of bed at 6am every morning, did his makeup and pulled on his black combat trousers. He loved those trousers – not only were they befitting of a rock star, they were also perfect for his role as a carer, incorporating as they did 14 various-sized pockets.

Contained within the side zip pockets were:

Brother (Don): heart medication (beta-blockers, statins and warfarin). Pacemaker information.

Mum (Mags): back medication (oral steroids, paracetamol and muscle relaxants).

Dad (Frank): catheter fixings and apparel.

Five: antidepressants (Mirtazapine 45mg).

A small plastic box containing wax earplugs.

. . .

Top pockets contained:

Repeat prescriptions.
   Hospital appointments.
   Benefits and pension books.
   Reminders to pay bills.
   A5 diary of social and band engagements.
   A5 notepad of song ideas, lyrics and plans for global rock domination, and a short list of telephone numbers of live music venues in Romford and Dagenham (only those where you are less likely to get your head kicked in for wearing eyeliner).

Back pockets contained:

Shopping lists.
   Weekly meal plans.
   A list of everyone's laundry days.
   Cleaning rota (with Five being the only person on the rota).

The term carer didn't adequately cover the multifarious permutations a role of this nature demanded. Five was a son, brother, cleaner, cook, financial adviser, concierge, walking family pharmacy, and only once had he accidentally put his trousers through the washing machine without emptying them. The routine was intense and with little in the way of respite, Five was forced to amuse himself by hiding his dad's only and beloved slipper in ever more creative places. This morning it was the fridge. Being a middle-aged man, his energy only carried him to about 7pm each day, when he fell to his knees knowing there were numerous jobs he hadn't had time to get to. One of the big problems he had was time. It evaporated faster than steam from a desert tea pot. Fitting in the band was always a struggle. Couple that with the problems him and Don were having with unreliable musicians and it was getting way too stressful. In the end it just made sense to get their mum and dad to join the band. Mags was classically trained and had played keyboards for a cabaret act at Pontins in the 1970s. She still used the same keyboard, which gave the band a unique edge in that it sounded a bit like a donkey farting in an echo chamber. They had almost saved up to buy her a new one last Christmas but the boiler broke down, so that scuppered that plan. Frank had played drums for a Fleetwood Mac covers band called Brentwood Mac, who were unfortunately as bad as the name suggested. He was forced to quit when he had his accident and so it was a little tricky now he was in a wheelchair, but they managed. Sort of.

Levering open the front door to take out the recycling, Five was body-slammed by what looked like the start of another gale. The lid had been blown off the bin and the front garden decorated with Tofurky meal packaging. Scrambling around on the front lawn in the Antarctic wind he soon lost sensation in his arms. He would have to fish the soya milk cartons out of the pond another day. Back in the sanctuary of the kitchen - with a precious ten minutes before getting everyone up, Five poured himself a cup of strong coffee and sat down at the breakfast table to plan the day. This was also an opportunity to indulge his favourite hobby of typing the words 'Obscure 1980s synth music' into YouTube and letting it run on automatic. In amongst the detritus there was nearly always a hidden gem of a tune that revealed itself and sent mini dopamine rushes whirling around his brain. One day, he hoped someone would discover his music in the same way.

The money was tight in the Watts household, not too tight to mention but if you did you might get a slap. With no one working and Five living off carer's allowance, it was nearly always a struggle. You only needed to look at the state of the place to see that. For a three-bed semi, the decor was state-of-the-art interior design – when it was last decorated in 1978. Frank was on his way to pay the builder when he had the motorbike accident that took his leg. The burnt orange geometric patterned wallpaper still hung as a memorial to that fateful day. To give the decor the illusion of choice, Mags referred to it as 'ashram chic' after reading an article about it in a magazine at the hairdressers. It was hard to update this kind of design without it looking like a student house, but they had at least been able to afford a new shag pile carpet and Don had a quote by the Buddha framed and placed above the TV. It read, 'Three words better than 'I love you' are 'I trust you'.

Today The Romford Bombers had come together to talk about the upcoming battle of the Numan tribute bands. Against Five's better judgment, he agreed to let Stubber facilitate the meeting using techniques he learnt in the Territorial Army. His life motto was 'Discipline is the difference between what you want now and what you want most.' He wasn't exactly sure what it meant but he was certain it was the cleverest thing he knew. Everyone was excited about hearing the special news that Tina had promised to reveal at the meeting, except for Five who was irritated she hadn't told him already. He would do his best to hide it, though, for fear of further inflaming the difficulties their relationship was currently experiencing.

Managing to disentangle himself from YouTube, he scampered up the stairs to haul his dad out of bed. Despite having a room on the north facing side of the house, Frank's room was always the warmest, defying the Alaskan heating sanctions imposed upon the rest of the house. Frank's explanation for this was that he had a body-heat disorder caused by excessive thyroxine which he attributed to a backstage party at a Fleetwood Mac gig in 1969. It allegedly involved illicit substances and a groupie's thigh. No one survives unscathed from the battlefield of rock. Frank was a gloriously hirsute man. He had long grey hair down his back and a wiry beard that had almost entirely colonized his face. Dragging him out of his bed of a morning was a bit like digging fluff out of your belly button, but far less satisfying. Five always had to endure the same argument.

'Another ten minutes.'

'You can't, I've got a tight schedule.'

'You're a little shit.'

Like I need this.

'I'm a busy little shit.'

'I'm not getting up.'

'Alright then, you can have cold porridge for breakfast and cook your own dinner.'

It was around this point in the proceedings that furball Frank materialized from deep within the eiderdown closely resembling cousin Itt from *The Addams Family*.

Following closely behind him as he glided down the stairlift, Five got him into his wheelchair and settled him down to breakfast. Then it was quickly back upstairs for the rest of them. Don and Mags normally only needed wake up calls unless Mags' back was playing up. That's when the manual handling course he did came in handy. Five knocked and entered his mum's room to find an empty bed. He then heard her voice coming from outside the front of the house.

'You can't park here!'

Five opened her bedroom window and stuck his head out to see her stood in the gutter in her dressing gown blocking the path of an irate man behind the wheel of a Vauxhall Corsa. *What the bloody hell are you doing, mum?*

'Why not?' said the man as he wound down the window.

'Because ambulances can't get in if there's an emergency, that's why not.'

'I've been driving round for half an hour looking for a space.'

'I know love but everyone in the street knows not to park here.'

'I can't see any fucking restrictions.'

'You could try round the back of the shopping centre—'

'I have, people are double parked back there.'

'My son's got a heart condition and he could need an ambulance at any time, we're all really worried 'bout him.'

'What's that got to do with me then?'

'It's only a matter of time before the council put down markings.'

'Until that 'appens, this is where I'm fucking parking, alright Grandma?' The man curled his lip, edging his Corsa forwards.

'I beg your pardon?' Mags' smile dropped in spectacular fashion.

Five came running out the house and tried to steer his mum away from the car but she was going nowhere.

'Are you gonna tell this bastard to scarper or am I gonna have to crawl up on his bonnet?'

The next thing they knew the man was half hanging out of his window with Stubber's leathery hand round his neck.

'You picking on a defenceless old lady, are you?

'Ahh, no... I'm sorry I was—'

'Do you fancy a piece of me instead?' Stubber clenched up his fist and placed it on the man's trembling chin.

'There's been a terrible misunderstanding,' the man spluttered, doing his best to look earnest.

Mags shuffled over and put her face close against the bedraggled looking guy.

'So you're fucking parking here, are you?'

'Not at all, I hope I didn't give you that impression.'

'Can you see how difficult it would be for the ambulance if you were parked here?'

'Absolutely, I completely understand.'

'Let him go, 'said Five trying to wrestle Stubber's grip from the man as his face slowly drained of colour.

'I'm sorry about this mate,' said Five, 'but it would make my life a lot easier if you could park somewhere else.'

Not requiring any further convincing, the guy slammed his car in reverse and made his retreat. Five ushered his mum – who was now almost frothing at the mouth – back into the house.

'How many times have I got to tell you? That's a battle you'll never win.'

'I'm never giving up on Don.'

'I'm with you there, Mags,' said Stubber, following behind them cracking his knuckles.

'No one's giving up on Don,' said Five. 'Go through to the front room, I'll get the kettle on. I'm leaving the door open for Tina.'

Frank was playing some drills with his drumsticks on the tattered arm of the leather sofa.

'Morning all, how's my beautiful wife today?'

Mags sat down next to him and gave him a big smacker on the lips.

'Me back's giving me a bit of gyp but I've just dosed up on Tramadol so I should be dandy soon.'

'You're a tough old bird Mags,' said Stubber, 'they don't make 'em like you anymore.'

'I could tell you some stories,' said Frank.

'And that'll be the last kiss you're getting off me.'

The Watts household had a shoes-off policy, but Stubber

wouldn't take his cowboy boots off for man nor beast. Apart from his wife Barbara, who was a Baptist minister and extremely particular about her hallway runner – a finely-woven depiction of the Last Supper, which Stubber mistook for a Led Zeppelin album cover. Someone on Twitter kindly pointed out his mistake after he'd tweeted a photo of it with the hashtag #metalminister. He grabbed the armchair and positioned it in front of the conservatory doors – centre stage – where he parked his backside and spread his tree trunk thighs so far apart it looked as though he was about to give birth. On went the Cartier designer glasses followed by a quick glance round to see who'd noticed. They say you can't buy class, so Stubber just nicked it instead. He couldn't recall who first gave him his nickname but he's adamant it dates back to when he was a chain smoker and had absolutely nothing to do with the fact he was five foot two. Only those with a sincere love of hospital food would dare suggest otherwise. He first became a roadie for the Romford Bombers ten years ago after seeing them, quite literally, bomb in a horrendous pub in Barking. At least, the place looked like a bomb had hit it after the crowd were done smashing the place up.

Five came back into the room, wobbling under a tray filled with pots of tea and a pack of budget ginger biscuits.

'Here you go everyone. I've been looking forward to today.' He hunched on the floor in the corner of the room as he refused to sit on the sofa on principle. If only they could afford some emergency chairs.

'I'm cream crackered,' said Stubber, rubbing the back of his neck. 'I was up all night.'

'I couldn't sleep either,' said Five. 'Those cranes were making weird noises again.'

'I was awake most of the night with my back,' said Mags. 'I never heard nuffin', it was bloody freezin' though love, can't we turn the heating up?'

Five grabbed a tartan blanket off the back of Stubber's armchair and launched it towards his mum.

'It will be even colder when they disconnect us.'

Mags cocooned herself and Frank, like a couple of barn owls.

'Have you been leaving that arm of yours alone?'

Five nodded, avoiding eye contact.

Flicking on the overhead lamp and positioning it so it lit himself up like a fairground attraction, Stubber relegated the rest of the room to a murky dusk.

Get your priorities straight Stubsy. Five got his notepad out and scribbled down the pertinent points he would need to raise at the meeting. The patter of gentle rain started to dance on the conservatory roof and a momentary stillness fell on the room as its inhabitants prepared themselves.

'Morning chums,' said Tina entering the room, 'how's it going?'

A smile erupted on Five's face, for the first time today, maybe all week.

With nowhere to sit and seemingly no gentlemen in the room, Tina slumped on the vector patterned carpet. She was wearing those patchwork leggings – that Five adored her in – even if was tricky to make out where her legs began and the carpet ended.

'Great to see you darling,' Five leant over and gave her a kiss on the forehead. 'Can't wait to hear this big news.'

'You're looking luverly, darlin,' said Frank.

'Thanks, hun,' said Tina, 'been getting down the gym a bit more lately.'

You never told me that, thought Five.

'I've not seen you in there,' said Stubber.

'I've started going to a new one called Frenchies in the High Street, women only. I got a bit bored of inhaling man-pits.'

'Can't imagine why,' said Mags, smiling.

Tina took her phone out of her pocket and swiped it open.

'So you all ready?'

Expectant wide eyes spread around the room.

'I had a chat with Candice from the fan club last night, I told her we were meeting today and she's kindly agreed to let us in on some top-level intel. It's good news and bad news I'm afraid.

'Give us the bad news first,' said Stubber, 'let's get it out the way.'

'Unfortunately, the Romford and Dagenham Gary Numan Fan Club is going into liquidation due to the economic downturn.'

Frank tutted and shook his head, like he was a leading financial analyst.

'That bloody downturn.'

'So as a final hurrah, they are hosting one more Battle of the Numan Tribute Bands to, this time, crown the all-time ultimate Gary Numan tribute act.'

'Amazing—' said Five. *This is our destiny.*

'Wait that's not all.' Tina paused to build the suspense. 'The winner will get to support Numan himself at the Royal Albert Hall in January.'

The room erupted, Five jumped to his feet and threw punches into the air.

'Jackpot!' shouted Stubber, giving Mags a high five.

'This is our moment folks, said Frank, 'I can feel it.'

'What will it mean if we get to support Numan?' said Mags.

Five positioned himself in the centre of the room for maximum effect.

'It means… the big time.'

'Easy tiger,' said Tina, 'we've gotta win it first.'

'Piece of piss,' Stubber astutely informed her before burping and filling the room with the delicate aroma of the sausage sandwich he'd devoured for breakfast. 'The Bombers are gonna fuckin' nail it.'

'So, if no one else knows yet, it means we've got an edge already.' Five scribbled something else in his notebook.

'Candice is announcing it at the fan club's party on Saturday night, so it would be a good idea for us to make an appearance, don't you think?' Tina tapped at Five's leg to get a response.

Five took in a deep breath, gave her the faintest of nods and knelt back down in the corner again.

Amidst the euphoria, Don's cosmic essence materialised in the doorway – a glowing apparition – his hands held against his mouth in prayer position.

Stubber immediately hopped to his feet.

'How you doing mate?' He grabbed a beanbag from the conservatory and plumped it up for him. 'You sit next to me.'

Don smiled and winked with both eyes. Everyone went quiet as he nestled into full lotus, like they were waiting for him to impart some transcendental wisdom, but that rarely happened before his first cup of coffee. He was a strict practitioner of mindful speech and only spoke when he truly believed he could improve on the silence. Or when Romford F.C. won a match. He was generally a very quiet man.

Stubber banged his vaporizer against an empty vase on the coffee table.

'Meeting in session. Did you all get the email I sent round?'

'I've been busy with my knitting.' Mags hunted under the cushions to find her bag of wool.

'I tried,' said Frank, 'but I couldn't find Google.'

Five could feel his jaw tighten. *Bloody hell.*

'It's a good job I printed off some copies innit?'

'Where are my glasses?' Frank reached over to his wheelchair to dig around in its crevices.

For fucks sake.

'Just talk us through it Stubsy, we'll be here forever.'

A second glance through his notes and an unnecessarily long throat clearance later, Stubber began.

'This meeting is all about defining our objectives. To get us started I'd like to ask a key question. Where are we going?'

'The gig's in London,' said Frank

'No, I mean, "What do we want to achieve?"'

'Recognition as serious artists,' said Five.

'We're a covers band,' Tina raised her eyebrows.

'Don and I have started writing our own songs, actually.'

'And they're bloody awful,' said Frank.

Shut up Dad, why don't you bloody well say something Don?

'Look,' said Stubber, tapping his vaporizer on his knee, 'if it's recognition we want, what do we need to do to achieve that?'

Tina pointed at Five. 'You really could improve on Numan's body movements, you're a bit wooden.'

Bollocks. 'I've studied Numan's body for 30 years, I know it better than he does—'

'Aye, I bet you have, but you stare at the floor too much. If you watch Ross onstage—'

'Don't you dare compare me to that amateur—'

'Didn't he win last year?'

'Maybe if you learnt to play the bass properly?' said Mags coming to the rescue of her son.

The room fell silent. The first drops of rain spat at the windows. Stubber ran his sleeve over his forehead. There was the rustle of Rizla papers as Frank rolled himself a cigarette. Mags found her knitting and cast on with her favourite loop technique. Tina checked the gossip on Facebook from her phone and Don radiated unconditional love from his bean bag whilst nibbling on a ginger nut. Five clambered to his feet and, without asking, poured top ups for anyone who needed it.

'The   bottom   line   is   that   we   need   to   beat   the

Stormtroopers.'

'Bastards,' growled Stubber.

'I saw Ross yesterday round the back of the undertakers, he was up to something weird.'

'That's just where he prepares the bodies,' said Tina looking up from her phone.

'He told me he did synth tech for Gary Numan,' said Mags.

'He does both.'

'Something wasn't right, they were dumping these red neon wires into a coffin.'

'He makes all kinds of electrical gadgets for tech competitions, he was probably just storing parts in a spare coffin.'

'How do you know so much about him?'

Tina flicked her eyes upwards before returning to her phone.

You can't answer that can you?

'I was wondering if it was him having me followed,' said Five.

'They might be planning to do you in,' said Stubber, making a gun shape with his hand. 'Maybe you should get some security cameras up?'

'You lot are living inside an episode of *The Twilight Zone*.' Tina pointed at Stubber. 'And you're wrong in the heid.'

'Could you sort that out, Stubsy?'

'Hang on,' said Mags, 'I'd need to OK that with the neighbours.'

'Creepy Jenny won't mind.'

'Is that the house with ripped curtains?'

'We used to go to school together, She's—'

'A lovely woman,' said Mags launching a ball of wool at her son. 'We don't mock the less fortunate in this house.'

'I was just—'

'Leave it.'

The rain was now so heavy it pummelled the conservatory

roof like a djembe drummer. Five looked up, worried it might start leaking again. Not only could they not afford to repair it; all their equipment was in there, it would be an utter disaster. Work on the industrial estate had kicked off for the day, pneumatic drills competed with dump trucks and high above it all were the cranes – moving like killer squid – their steel tentacles, stretching and screeching under the weight of Progress.

'Why don't we get a couple of dancers like Bucks Fizz used to have? asked Mags

'I'll come on and pull their skirts off,' said Stubber leaning forward.

'You old perv,' said Tina

'It's not me training to become a sex therapist is it?'

'How's your wife these days? Still shagging behind her back are yer?'

'We have an open relationship actually.'

'Aye, but does she know about that?'

'We share everything we need to.'

'I'm sure you talk about your feelings all day long.' Tina puffed out her chest to mimic him. '"Barbara, I had two 20-year-old groupies in bed last night and for the life of me I couldn't decide which one to do first."'

'I always know that,' said Stubber.

'You know what your issue is don't yer?'

''Ere we go….'

Rolling off his bean bag, Don got up and quietly wafted out the room, returning to safer pastures. This kind of negativity can really mess with your mindfulness.

'You're scared of the vagina,' said Tina. 'That's why you seek to denigrate women.'

Stubber's legs started to slowly draw inwards like a pair of canal gates closing.

Frank leant forward and put his hand on Tina's shoulder. 'Have some respect love.'

'Respect? Tell that old fuck badger to find some respect for women, then I'll show him some respect. How about that?'

'I can't help it, I've got a hypersexual disorder, it's a syndrome.'

'Sounds serious,' said Tina.

Stubber's legs fused together as he fumbled about in his kit bag, clearly unsure what he was looking for.

This time Tina kicked Five in the leg. 'Why aren't you sticking up for me?'

'I'm not getting involved.' He lent back against the wall. He could feel the vibration of the cranes through the bricks, it seemed to reach deep inside him. He pulled up a tartan blanket so he could scratch his arm in secret.

'You never do.' Tina got up and put her jacket on.

Don't leave.

'Where you going?'

'I've gotta get my car to the garage, it needs a service.'

'So does your boyfriend,' said Frank following up with a drum roll on the armrest of the sofa.

Tina glared at Five. 'That's fucking great. Do you tell everyone what's going on with us?'

'We're a close family.' Five stared at the floor.

'Aye, there's close and then there's weird mate.'

'Don't call me mate.'

Tina picked up her bag and marched out the house.

'Cheers for winding her up everyone.' Five threw his notebook across the living room. 'That's just what I need right now.'

Frank emptied his nose into a handkerchief. 'Fink I'm coming down with sumfing.'

Mags pushed herself up onto her walking stick. 'I need a lie down.'

'Fuck this,' said Stubber. 'I'm going to check on Rambo.'

Five walked slowly down the hallway to his ice-cold box room. He put his headphones on and lay down on his bed. The time was 10.35am and the day was already over.

TEXT AND MAKE UP

Five

How did it go? X 10:36

Tina

Making a funny noise (car not me) Then had all that college
work, knackered (me not car) 10:41

Five

Sorry about earlier X 10:46

Tina

Talk about it tomorrow 10:48

Five

Love you X 10:49

Tina

Night mate x 10:49

FRANK'S BLOWER

Frank

I.NEED.AN.EXTENSION.LEAD.FOR.
THE.HEATER. HE'S. GETTING.SUSPICIOUS.
I.WANNA.MOVE.IT. ROUND.BACK.OF.BED 08:24

Mags

How am I supposed to get one? 08:51

Frank

SAY.ITS.FOR.YOUR.SOWING.MACHINE.
AND.THAT.I'VE.OFFERED.TO.PAY.
FOR.IT 08:55

Mags

He'll never believe that! 09:06

Frank

DO.YOU.LIKE.BEING.WARM? 09:12

Mags

I'll do it. 09:21

3

THE ABYSS

27th October

Winter had come early. It had hit Romford like a blunt force trauma, its icy jackboots lumbering over the town's veins and arteries, laying trip wires and setting time bombs. The elderly were being hit the hardest, the community centres were nearly deserted and Meals on Wheels were reporting a 50% increase in customers failing to answer their front doors. The forecast said it was being caused by changes in the position of the jet stream, whatever that meant. One thing was for sure, if it was like this in October you knew you were in it for the long haul. None of it was very likely to lighten your mood, especially if you were inclined to take it personally. Five read the weather forecast as if it were a letter from an old friend who no longer wanted to see him. The rain bothered him the most, its relentless dirge rattled his soul and fed his already compulsive tendency toward introspection.

Five slept – when able – in a room downstairs on the

north-facing side of the house, which was originally built as a utility room and had what's known in the trade as a single-skin wall. The wind seeped through its bricks like blood through the grids of an abattoir floor. It was still the only room in the house with plumbing for a washing machine so he was stuck with it. He had his record player on top of it as way of reclaiming the space and it kind of worked; he just couldn't use them both at the same time.

The delectable Miss Tina Clark had graced Five with her presence before going out for lunch-time drinks with friends. Five wasn't invited. She sat at his dressing table, trowelling a thick layer of foundation onto her pitted face and, despite the temperature, was wearing her lacey black blouse, cut deep at the sides to reveal just enough bra to destabilise Five. He lay back on the bed and tried desperately not to steal mini, clandestine glances over at her. Those glorious arms, hanging like velvet curtains – purple sheened and rippling with goose-bumps – were capable of cradling away any human misery.

The washing machine clicked and gurgled as its barrel filled with water.

'Your tea's gonna go cold, sure you don't want a sarnie?'

'We're gonna get some scran there. Can we get some daylight in here?' Tina's breath turned to frost as she spoke.

Five frowned, opened the curtains – no wider than ten centimetres – then sat down on his bed.

'I've written a new song.'

'Yeah?'

'I saw this documentary on these twins being reunited after thirty years…it really moved me.'

'That's sweet.'

'It's…' – Five met Tina's eyes in the dressing table mirror – 'about rekindling lost love.'

Tina looked away and checked the time on her phone. 'Can you do my hair at the back?'

A rare chance for some physical contact. Five grabbed a comb and stretched out a big handful of jet black hair as wide as he could manage.

'Careful, that hurts.' Tina glanced up at him. 'Yours is sticking up at the back again too.'

'It needs redoing, can't afford it right now.' Five then launched into a back-combing session that was so enthusiastic it ended with Tina looking like she'd stuck her fingers in the mains socket. 'That looks better.' He put the comb down and softly stroked her forearm. Inhaling deeply, he then bent down and kissed her tenderly on the shoulder.

'Leave it out mate,' she flinched and brushed his hand away. 'I've got a killer headache.'

'You're still going out though?'

'It's a college thing, I can't cancel.'

'Who with?'

'No one you know.'

You expect me to believe that? Five flopped back on the bed. 'I'm sorry about the meeting,'

'You know there's a lot you all avoid talking about, don't you?'

'Like what?'

'The fact you sound like Stars on 45 doing Numan.'

'That's not fair. At least we play the songs in same key and tempo as Numan. We never hit a note wrong.'

'What about your mum's keyboards?'

'Like we can afford a decent synth?'

'Can't Stubber get hold of one?'

Five smiled, 'you mean nick one?'

'Yer ain't gonna beat The Storm Troopers sounding like that, they're too professional.'

'Course we will, anyway what's all this 'you' business?'

Tina filled the air with pound shop hair spray that smelt of glue and paraffin. The wash cycle banged, whirred, sloshed.

'Your tea is gonna go cold,' said Tina pointing at the mug, 'You up for the party at Candice's house on Saturday then?'

Absolutely not.

'Who's going?'

'The usual suspects.'

'I'm a bit anxious about it.'

'Aye you normally are.' Tina pouted and applied a thick lashing of crimson red lipstick. 'You know her dad is one of the judges this year?'

'I had a panic attack at last year's party.'

'Ross is going.'

That really helps.

'How do you know?'

'Linda off my course is mates with him, he's nae as bad as you all make him out to be.'

'He fancies you, of course he's nice.'

Tina avoided his eyes in the mirror and applied another layer of mascara. 'He's actually got a very serious illness, we're not sure what it is but Linda fears the worst. I think he might show his face today, actually.'

Is that why you're getting so dressed up?

Five took a clean pair of combats out of his drawers and quickly swapped trousers. The sting of the cold metal zip upon his skin offered a momentary respite to the tightness in the pit of his stomach. He then picked up his battered acoustic guitar and played the opening riff to The Joy Circuit. An attempt to summon the spirit of Numan. Someone who would never let him down.

'Anyway, I'll have to see how mum's back is on Saturday, it's been playing her up lately.'

'You should hear yersel', yer a wee bain, you've never left home and never grown up.'

Here we go.

'You promised me we'd get a flat together years ago.'

'Who would look after everyone?'

'You take on far too much for them.'

'Can we go to the party together?'

'They are much more capable than they let on.'

'I can't go my own'

'If Mags can play online bingo, she can do online shopping.'

'She tried and ordered 55 loo rolls by mistake.'

'Your nae coping.'

'I'm doing my best… you don't know what it's like.'

'The whole world is wearing a Halloween mask as far you are concerned.'

The screech and roar of the spin cycle pierced the air and Five winced. It rang in A minor, the same key as Five's tinnitus. The vibration sent Tina's make up to rolling onto the floor. Five got down on his knees to pick it up.

'It didn't happen to you.'

It may as well have…yer letting it take you over…it's turning yer odd.'

'I've always been different.'

'That's nae what I mean and you know it, you think someone's following yer for god's sake… the scratching is getting worse too'

'I hardly do that anymore.'

'Look at your bedsheets, they're like a box of weetabix.'

Five stared at the floor, lost for words.

'Drink your tea.' Tina swivelled round on her seat to face Five. 'I *do* love you ...'

Why are you saying it like that?

'I know you do.'

'But I cannae watch you destroy yersel.'

'What are you saying?'

'I made promises to my dad.'

'What's that got to do with me?'

'You're pulling me down with you. Is that what you want?'

The sound of stretching steel reverberated outside the window. Five walked over to the window and closed the curtains.

'What's up with that?'

He didn't reply.

'See it's stuff like that I'm talking about... weird mate.'

'Stop calling me mate.'

'Anyway, I'll be working late in the library on Saturday, I'll see you at the party.'

Five climbed into bed and pulled the genuine eiderdown duvet over his lap. Stubber had got it for his last birthday and it was probably worth more than the house. He dreaded to think what lorry it had fallen off. He had very nearly given it back but it was just way too warm. Morality can be a messy business.

Tina stood up and flung her bright red PVC trench coat around her shoulders.

'Come and give me a hug.' Five tried to beckon her with his eyes.

'No time, see you at the party?'

'I'm not going on my own.'

'It's just a party for fuck's sake.' Tina clacked her tongue piercing against the back of her teeth.

No response.

'Alright mate, whatever,' she turned on her heels and strutted out of the door.

The washing machine whimpered as it came to the end of its cycle. The crotch of Frank's pants had stuck to the glass portal, clinging on like an alien life-form. Five picked up his mug and took a slurp of stone-cold tea which he spat out over his eiderdown. He then ripped back the covers, sprang to his feet and sprinted to the front door just as Tina was disappearing into the encroaching fog. He screamed as loudly as he could, 'STOP FUCKING CALLING ME MATE.'

He stood waiting...staring into the abyss...but the only

response came from the piercing lights of the cranes as they hauled iron girders towards the heavens.

4

ZEBEDEE AND THE GREEN FAIRY

1st November, 10 a.m.

The last of the morning chores had been completed. Mags and Frank were reacquainting their ample behinds with the sofa and Five was pouring boiling hot tea from a cracked china pot. Insidious dross spewed from a TV chat show and the hollow thud of rain jabbed at the conservatory's brittle polycarbonate roof. The antiquated cuckoo clock in the hall chimed ten times, prompting Five to lay out his mum's medication on the coffee table. The morning was as familiar as it was agitating.

'I'm making you something to wear on stage for the tournament,' said Mags, picking up a bright yellow ball of wool and yanking the needles out of it.

Fuck me.

'I look forward to that mum'

'Stubber got it me. No questions…'

What a bastard.

'Right.'

'Me and your mum have been talking,' said Frank whilst scanning the front room for his slipper. 'We think Tina's letting the band down.'

Not this again.

'She tries her best.'

'We know love and she's still bloody useless,' said Mags as she cast on.

'Can we talk about this later? I'm off to see Pete before the party.'

'How's he getting on?' asked Mags.

'Alright… I think.'

'Whatever happened about him getting arrested for shagging that tramp?' asked Frank before blowing his nose with a fragile-looking tissue.

'He was arrested for having sex in public.'

'With a tramp?' Frank studied the contents of the tissue.

'He was a homeless man.'

'Why would anyone want to shag someone that's homeless?' asked Mags.

''Cause he found him attractive?'

'Why didn't they just go to bed?'

'That's when Pete was homeless as well.' *I'm gonna get shit-faced tonight.*

'Oh, I understand now, I think,' said Mags

'Why did he get arrested then?' asked Frank.

With a gentle shake of his head, Five walked out of the front door and put his coat on in the rain. He sidled across the lawn, lifted up the lid of the compost bin and – with a gang of expectant worms looking up at him – dropped in his dad's slipper.

The fog had given way to a fine drizzle, sending anyone daft enough to be outside, inside. Droplets of water hung like diamonds from the cobwebs under creepy Jenny's window. Her curtains twitched as he walked past and an eye appeared through a tear in the rotting fabric.

His chest tightened and legs weakened but he kept his head straight and marched on towards the sanctuary of the bus shelter at the end of the road. Truth be known he felt abandoned by Jenny. They were very close once. She used to stick up for him when the class skinhead screamed 'queer freak' in his face in the canteen. As if school dinners weren't bad enough. She went on to become a successful makeup artist, working with famous musicians. She even went on tour with Numan for a while before locking herself away. That was about five years ago now. Since then Mags was the only person she'd have any contact with. Five found it all very unsettling. Perhaps his fear was that one day he may end up like her.

After quite a few years of nomadic truth seeking – roughing it in anarchist squats across London – citizen Pete now kept it real by living in a three-by-four metre mobile home in his mum's back garden. Under the radar, he spent his days working as an autonomous digital nomad, white hat hacker committed to exposing corruption with every click of his mouse. He played no part in society's devastating reliance on fossil fuels and as such lived almost completely off-grid. It's just the one extension lead he runs from the garage into his serving hatch where his mum leaves his dinners for him. Come winter freeze or summer heat, he was committed to enduring any hardship for the good of humanity. Apart from January and February that is, when he stayed in his mum's spare room.

Today, Five had a couple of favours to ask Pete, that's if he managed to gain entry. It was impossible trying to remember the complex knocking code he'd been given. *Was it two knocks then wait, then three more? Or the other way around?*

'Who's there?' Pete's gravelly voice could be heard from behind the door.

'It's me.'

'Do the knock.'

'I can't remember it, just look through the spy hole.'

'You could be disguised to look like you.'

'Let me in you twat, I'm freezing.'

There was the clank of multiple locks opening before Pete's crusty face appeared, 'I'm on code red at the moment brother.'

Five couldn't help noticing the ten new water butts linked to Pete's roof and before he could stop himself he'd blurted, 'What are they for?'

'Do you know the government can kill us all with the flick of a switch?'

Why do I do it to myself?

'Everyone knows that over 80% of our tap water is contaminated with micro-plastics, right? But what they don't know is that some of it is autonomous nanotechnology, specifically mini explosives planted and controlled by the government.'

'Really?' The floor creaked under Five's boots as he walked into the room.

'Straight up, take old Albert next door, last summer he took out *The Communist Manifesto* from the library on a Friday. On the Saturday morning he was earthing up his potatoes and lit up his back garden like a bloody Catherine wheel.'

Five ground his teeth in a desperate bid not to smile.

'His wife reckons it was spontaneous human combustion, but that's a bit paranoid if you ask me.' Pete pointed over to the two half-melted wellington boots in the corner of the room. 'Look what I fished out of her recycling.'

Pete's take on home decor was a somewhat minimalist interpretation in that it dispensed with the decor part of the equation. The multi-layered tin foil covering the walls and windows performed a dual function: protection from electromagnetic rays and support for the illusion that Pete lived inside the Nebuchadnezzar. Five had never plucked up the courage to ask him if he thought he was Morpheus or Neo. The one picture he did have was a framed album cover of

Aladdin Sane, signed by the man himself. Pete's morning ritual normally began with kissing the picture before turning on his laptop and drinking a mug of coffee so strong it could wake the dead.

All subversive operations were carried out from a vast desk that Pete fished out of a skip in the industrial park. It took up nearly 60% of the room and around 99% of Pete's waking life. Wedged alongside the desk was a manky old futon which you had to climb over in order to get to the toilet. Judging by the smell of it you could surmise there have been a good few occasions when he just hadn't bothered. Pete lit an incense cone sending a thick plume of sandalwood spiralling toward the ceiling.

Not wanting to contaminate his freshly washed combats, Five managed to squat on the futon holding a comb and compact mirror as he set to work on his stubborn ridge of hair.

'Got any hair spray?'

'That stuff will make you even more flammable,' Pete waved his hand dismissively.

'What you working on then?'

'I'm balls deep in the dark web, brother.' Pete sat down at his desk and pointed at his laptop. 'I'm making connections with some high level anarcho-hackers. We're gonna form a collective and bring the whole corrupt house of cards tumbling down. That's if I can keep the benefits officer off my back, do you know he tried to get me a job as a Portaloo cleaner? Imagine driving round in a truck full of shit all day long?'

'Beggars belief,' said Five, trying not to laugh again.

'How's things with Tina?'

'You know… awful.' Five spat into the palm of his hand and used it to smear his hair down. 'I think she's been hanging round with that Ross. There's something well dodgy about that bloke.'

'How so?'

'This time last year no one in the Numan fan club had heard of him or his band, even though he supposedly works for Numan and has been working at the undertakers. He reckons he started The Storm Troopers up three weeks before last year's competition but they didn't hit a single note wrong. It took us years to get to that stage. Tell me that's not weird.'

'They are bloody good musicians, though.'

'What are you saying?' Five's eyebrows dipped inwards.

'Nothing brother—'

'The thing is, the tournament rules are very clear. All the acts need to have done at least 25 gigs in order to qualify. Where is the evidence they've done that?'

'Want me to have a little dig around, see if there's any dirt?'

'It won't be traceable if we do, will it?' Five nibbled at the quick of his finger whilst attempting not to chip his nail varnish.

'I'm a virtual ghost,' Pete winked at him and rubbed his hands together like Dick Dastardly before carefully peeling open his laptop. 'Welcome to the online underworld of Zebedee Mind Love.'

'Huh?'

'It's my handle, brother...'

Five squinted.

'Never mind, what's his surname?'

'Patterson, but go easy, Tina reckons he's sick.'

Pete nodded as he typed.

'Leave it with me.'

'You coming to the party tonight?'

'Nah, I'm gonna do an all-nighter.'

'Oh, go on, you know how nervous I get at these things?'

'Why don't you stay here with me? I'm trying out this new love medicine.'

'I'd love to mate but it's gonna be ram packed with Numanoids tonight and it's important to put in an appearance, make a good impression before the tournament, know what I mean?'

'Tina will be there won't she?'

'She's always off talking to people… why don't you come and be my wingman, just like old times?'

Pete looked up from his laptop with a sheepish expression.

'Truth is brother… I'm banned from Candice's house.'

'She will have forgotten about it by now.'

'I don't think so… I had a bit of a disastrous ménage à trois at her place last month which I think she deeply regrets.'

'How do you know?'

'It was with her mum and dad.'

Five sunk his face into his hands.

'That's just wrong! Her dad's one of the judges this year.'

Pete grinned and picked up a biro lid to pick a bit of museli out of his teeth.

'I don't think I'll go then, what happens if I have another panic attack?'

Pete reached an arm around him.

'Why don't you try some of what I'm taking? It will chill you right out.'

'Will it work?' Five had the sneaking suspicion he already knew the answer.

'I found out about it from an online pal who told me everyone's doing it over in the U.S. It's called a tampon love bomb, you soak a tampon in meths then stick it up your arse, it's the fastest route to the brain, see. I'm using 70% proof absinthe instead.'

'I'll be off my tits.'

'No brother, you just won't give a fuck about nuffin. Do you know what this absinthe is also known as?'

Five shook his head looking more than a little concerned.

'The Green Fairy' – Pete put his face up to Five's and widened his eyes to owl proportions – 'coz that's who you meet when you drink it.'

'Tina will think I've lost it.'

'And why do you care what she thinks?'

'You're right... I'm always bending over for her.'

Pete reached down into a plastic tub under his desk and presented him with a dripping wet tampon.

'Bend over for this instead, brother... I've been marinating it for two weeks.'

Five took a deep breath in and ambled off to the bathroom. The caravan fell silent, save for the clickety clack of Pete's battered keyboard. Despite failing visibility and oxygen levels, Pete lit another incense cone and dabbed a couple of drops of patchouli oil under his armpits. A glass of bright blue liquid glimmered in the light from the computer screen which he downed in one before grunting and sticking his face back into the portal of his digital underworld.

There was a tap at the door.

'Hello dear?'

It was Pete's mum. She'd not been giving him much peace lately due to her wild notion that he may have an internet addiction. Hence the random spot checks. Pete was bloody furious about it, especially after telling her to email before coming over. He stopped typing until she gave up and scurried back off up the path to the bungalow.

All was quiet in the bathroom, right up until a shrill voice blurted out from behind the door, 'It's stuck!'

Pete put his head to the door. 'Didn't you leave the string side hanging out?'

'You never told me to!'

'I thought it would be obvious!'

'Like I do this every day!'

'Don't worry brother, it'll be a better rush and you'll poop it out tomorrow anyway.'

Five waddled out of the bathroom, wafting the smoke out of his face. He picked up his mirror and with one last wistful glance pinned his baseball cap firmly to his head.

'You promise this is going to be alright?'

Pete gave him a bear hug.

'Just tune in to your inner Zen and you'll be floating all night.'

Already the neurons were flashing in his brain, 'I need to dance.' Five pointed at Pete's record collection.

'Music, maestro!'

'Yes brother!' Pete swung round on his chair and huddled his bony frame over his album collection that was neatly arranged in packing crates next to his desk. He rifled through it, animatedly pulling an album out only to um and ah before moving onto the next contender. Choosing the perfect song to capture a special moment between two old buddies shouldn't be taken lightly. And there was no better medium than vinyl, the raw spirit of music in its primal form. After all, that's what being in a band should be about – disaffected radicals screaming their anger at the world. Subverting the dominant paradigms and – much to Stubber's horror – disrupting the status quo.

Five leaped over the futon and found himself a small section of wonky floor big enough to dance on.

With the perfect album chosen, it was carefully placed on the turntable.

The needle was slowly lowered onto the vinyl.

There was the amplified crackle of dust in the groove.

The tingle of anticipation.

A whoosh of endorphins.

The dizzy spin of blood tearing through veins.

Pete took his place on the futon, flailing his arms through the fog of incense in preparation.

Then, blaring out from the speakers came the opening riff of The Prodigy's 'Fire Starter'. They stomped and spun, twisted and curled as this intoxicating tune wormed its way through their auditory canals. Pete looked like he was praying to some wrathful deity, while Five used his index fingers to paint infinity loops in the incense. They were lost in the possibilities of another world. A world where this room was on board the Nebuchadnezzar. A world where Five was on stage in front of thousands of devoted fans. And, as the song reached its crashing climax, he realised that it was a world that had allowed him – for a few blissful minutes – to forget himself.

5

DON'T TAKE MYSTERY TO BED

1st November, 6 p.m.

The number 499 bus to Gallows Corner came roaring down the street, leaving a light trail in its wake. Five grabbed the support rail and hoisted himself inside about as nimbly as someone wearing a 1950s diving suit.

'Chatteris Avenue please.'

There were two Numanoids he recognised at the back of the bus, – but social anxiety being what it is – he was up those stairs in a jiffy. Naturally there was only one seat available, in the worst possible place too. The row *in front* of the back row. The creep seats. Five attempted to merge as innocuously into his surroundings as possible, given the fact a burning numbness was eating away at his brain. *What the fuck has he given me?*

Behind him, stretched out on the back row, sat three young men. They were motionless with hoods dangling down over their heads like the Black Riders from Mordor. The only clue that they might have been sentient life forms was from the glare of their phone screens illuminating their vacuous expressions.

Fumbling around in his trouser pockets, Five managed to locate his phone but not his glasses. The screen was nothing more than a blur as he jabbed blindly at the security code. *Why did she set this up for me?* At the fifth attempt he got lucky and scrawled a text message to Tina, 'R U therre yety?' He checked his back pocket for his emergency paper bag he'd stored earlier. *Maybe I could just get some chips and go home… she would call me a wuss … I've got to go.*

He wiped his moist palms on the bus seat and checked his make-up in his compact mirror. Sweat had got into his eyes and was making his eyeliner form little black torrents down his face. *I look like Alice Cooper… I need my foundation.*

An older man in the seat in front began enthusiastically whistling a shrill rendition of Vera Lynn's 'We'll Meet Again'.

Five gripped the side of his bus seat.

Behind him Black Rider one grunted to his companion, 'Ow long you been out?'

'Two days,' replied Black Rider two, not looking up from his phone.

'A bit of bird never done ya any 'arm, 'ey?'

'A wing was well lively bruv, my cellmate was stabbed in the face, I'm telling ya.'

Five's knuckles were turning white and a nausea was sweeping over him. *Just breathe, just breathe.*

The lady in the seat opposite – also submerged in her phone – took a while to notice her young son slurping milk-shake through a straw and blowing it onto the back of the bus seat. The pink froth sprayed across the aisle and decorated Five's combats. Not the most sociable of gestures, especially abhorrent to a vegan.

'Cut it out, that's gross,' the mother cuffed the boy round the head.

Black Rider three, obviously a maverick, had decided to

use his phone for the bizarre purpose of making a phone call. 'Bruv, you got what we need?'

The bus pulled into Pettits Lane. Five wiped the condensation from the window and looked for solace in the outside world. Rain corralled in little silver bubbles before bursting and forming estuaries that zigzagged down the window. Distant lights made red blurry fractals like bullet holes in the glass, he realised these were from the cranes, so quickly brought himself back into the bus.

'You giv' us da money yeh?' Black Rider three was starting to lose his shit.

A needle-like pain registered in the crease of Five's arm. He looked down to see himself clawing at it again. *How can I not realise I'm doing it?*

The Vera Lynn concerto in front was now hitting a crescendo, as the man raised his arms to conduct his finale. The pitch of his whistle was like a knitting needle to Five's eardrums which only added to the feeling his brain was melting. It would surely only be a matter of time before it started dribbling out of his nose.

'We're comin' to ya fackin' yard.' Black Rider three started punching the back of Five's seat.

The little boy sucked up the last of his milkshake and sprayed it all over his mother in a stealth revenge attack.

'You little shit!'

The overhead lights flashed. Suddenly there was no oxygen. The aisle between the seats began to open up. He yanked out his paper bag as the bus tannoy announced, 'The next stop will be Chatteris Avenue.'

Thank fuck for that.

He dragged his DMs along the sodden street like a teenager on his way to school. A budget can of cider carried on foamy rapids rattled its way down the gutter. Up ahead, the music blared and the lights glimmered as groups of friends huddled under umbrellas, laughing as they rushed up the garden path towards the party. Five would have rather been anywhere else in the entire universe than here. It wasn't that he didn't know everyone at the party, it was just that to call them friends would be pushing it. All those years when The Bombers were the top band, all of Essex's most fervent Numanoids wanted to hang out with him. They would tag him in photos on Facebook. He would get invited to every party and put on every guest list. He virtually had the keys to Romford, well Dagenham at least. Admittedly, he was too shy to attend any of these events, but it was very nice to be invited. Not that it happens anymore. Now the best he got was a cursory, pitying nod, a vague acknowledgement of somebody they used to know. Like an old sheep dog whose legs have gone and has no other propose than to wait for the farmer to arrive with his shotgun. That was the fickle world of entertainment and that was why it was vital The Bombers won this year. Five knew everything would be OK again when that happened.

He sat on the garden wall and stared up at Candice's mock Tudor house. His heart beat in time with the music that clattered its windows. He mooched over to the front of the house and noticed the new wooden engraved plaque above the door, 'Romford and Dagenham Gary Numan Fan Club - Head Quarters.' He raised his hand to press the bell but instead found himself turning around and scuttling back down the garden path. Before he could make his escape, though, the silver tones of Candice's larynx rang out behind him.

'Oi oi saveloy!'

She was everybody's favourite host; the fact that she was the only one who bothered to host anything was just a coincidence. Tonight she was tarted up like a stick of Brighton rock but nowhere near as classy.

'Where you off to, you muppet?'

'Oh...I just thought... I'd dropped something.'

Five navigated the journey back up the path like he was walking the plank.

'You look brown.'

'Just back from Ibeefa babe, bit of winter sun, know what I mean?' She gave him her enormous trademark smile. A smile that seemed disproportionate to the amount of happiness you suspected she had for seeing you. It was not a disagreeable smile, however, and her plump lips were sanguine with curves reminiscent of Antoni Gaudí's architecture. Each end of her smile propped up two shallow dimples just deep enough to be filled by a single tear. But it was her mouth's internal structure that really stole the show. For if anything could be said for Candice, it was that she had fantastic teeth. Everybody said so. They were moulded like marble tomb stones, perfectly equidistant and as white as summer clouds. If ever a statement could be said to contain objective truth, it was that Candice Bamford had a sterling crop of knashers.

Possessing the elevated position of chairperson of the fan club, she presided over these parties with the air of an aristocrat, – her Christian Louboutin heels, Chanel handbag and 2,300 Instagram followers – all social proofs of her standing. If only her eyes didn't reveal a fear that no one else recognised her significance.

Five embraced her with an awkwardness that only comes from hugging someone you don't know well enough to hug.

'We're back to our best again this year,' he blurted out, making sure to set out his stall from the off.

'You better had be, I saw the Storm Troopers rehearse yesterday and they were fackin' amazing.' Candice applied a fresh lashing of lipstick via her porch window reflection. 'Their singer's a luverly bloke too ain't he? Gave my Lance a right good deal on his mum's burial.'

That sounds like a bribe to me. I must read the tournament rulebook again.

'Have you picked a second judge yet?'

'My dad's got his best mate in, Mr Morris. I'm not even joking, but he's proper uptight yeah?'

'He didn't used to be a geography teacher by any chance?'

'That's the one. Anyway must mingle. Help yourself to drinks.' Candice fluttered off to resume her hosting duties.

Five draped his dripping wet coat over the banister and poked his head into the front room. The place was rammed, the music ear-splitting. He decided it prudent to pop in some wax earplugs; he didn't want his tinnitus getting any worse. They are also useful for tuning out drunken bullshit.

Tina appeared in front of him, sweat pouring down her face.

'Great music!'

'I called *and* texted you.'

'Aye, I was chatting to Ross.'

'Why?'

'It's a party?'

Five stood stock-still, staring at Tina, his eyeliner smeared across his face. 'Have you got my foundation?'

'Why don't you try and fucking enjoy yourself for once?' She turned on her bootheels and disappeared again into the throng of sweaty black-clad bodies jumping around in the front room.

The staircase looked a good place to get his head together. It had pink shagpile carpet and looked more comfortable than his bed. He sat down carefully, placing his weight on his right buttock for fear of getting any deeper into trouble with Pete's love bomb. Apart from the hostile drum beat of his heart he now had very little sensation from the neck down and a strong suspicion he was melting into the carpet. He was annoyed at himself. He should have learnt this lesson when they were at school. Like the time Pete convinced him to have a hash brownie before a chemistry class in which they had to perform the elephant toothpaste experiment. It didn't end well. A line of drool slipped out of the corner of his mouth into the carpet. He leaned back to try and calm his spinning head. In front of him the hallway light was eclipsed as a tall figure approached him.

'Alright, Five?'

And there he was – all six foot five of him – Ross Patterson. The man with more front than Margate. Swaggering down the hall with his army boots, steel jaw line and upper body strength. He looked like a cross between a Smurf and an Action man that had been left out in the sun too long. Following closely behind him, weighing in at about a third of his size, was the Storm Troopers' bass player. A man who had been assembled from a DIY kit consisting only of black hair dye, crimpers and Bauhaus lyrics. To complete the persona, he had a laugh like a constipated yeti. Five had given him the nickname 'the Count' though, after due consideration, felt quite strongly the name had one letter 'o' too many.

Ross checked his reflection in a picture frame and ran his hands through his brand new hair transplant. He'd gone for the Berserker look and dyed it electric blue. He grinned and gave himself a knowing wink. When you're this good looking, why feign modesty?

Five shrugged his shoulders.

'Like that, hey?' Ross lit up a cigarette and sent a cloud of smoke up the stairs. 'They're a bunch of fucking dead weights here aren't they?'

'Huh Huh,' snickered the Count.

'It reminds me of the time when me and Numan went to this party during the Savage tour.' Ross lent down towards Five. 'Have you ever met Gary?'

'Nearly,' said Five tightening his face. 'I was at a record signing, I was next in the queue but he had to leave.'

You knew that already.

'Coz you know I'm their keyboard technician, don't you?'

What a tosser.

'I don't think you have ever mentioned it before,' Five exhaled, rattling his lips.

'Anyway, I pretended to be Numan for a laugh, everyone believed it, Gary was cracking up.'

'Huh Huh.'

'I bet he pissed himself,' said Five. 'Anyway I'll meet him when we support him next year.'

'You know about that already do you? Think you've got what it takes to be King Numanoid then?'

'What, compared to you?

Ross winked at the count. 'How sweet is that? It's healthy to have a positive mental attitude... despite everything.'

I'd love to spit in his face.

Five didn't reply and instead dug around in his combats looking for his compact mirror.

'Speaking of keyboards, has your mum still got her keyboard? Good bit of kit that. How does she get that foghorn sound?'

'Huh, huh.'

'Least she can play,' said Five. 'Anyway we might go back to just guitars like Tubeway Army.'

Ross squinted.

'You do know they started out as a guitar band?'

'Yeah... 'course.' Avoiding Five's eyes, Ross took his phone out of his pocket and started typing something.

How does he not know that?

'Sod this.' Picking himself up, Five set off in the hope of finding civilisation and, more importantly, coffee.

Ross stubbed his cigarette on the banister railing while adjusting his crotch. He glanced at the count and, raising an eyebrow, murmured, 'I hope we don't have any problems with him.'

'Let's keep an eye on him,' came the reply.

'So we gonna give these losers a little nudge in the right direction then?'

'Huh huh.'

'Make sure no one's watching.' Ross strutted back into the front room, running his hands through his hair. He paused briefly to smile at Tina, which she responded to with a frantic fluttering of eyelashes. Sidling over to the drinks table and with the Count close behind, he took out a bag of ground up Viagra and emptied it into the punch bowl.

Neither coffee nor anything resembling hospitable life-forms could be found, so Five made the executive decision to give up and go find Tina instead. He squeezed his way through the mass of bodies blocking the kitchen door and found himself presented with the very last thing he felt able to deal with – Tina dancing with Ross. They were gyrating their hips in sync to the rampant beats of Electric Six's 'Danger! High Voltage' and staring deep into each other's eyes. It was almost soft porn. She was doing her goofy laugh that sounded like she had hiccups. A laugh that used to be reserved for him.

The Count made them pose for photos – which they did a bit too eagerly, throwing their arms around each other. Five took a seat next to the drinks table and wished all manner of evil atrocities upon both of them. *Those horrible bastards.* He had now given up hope of ever finding the promised land of inner Zen and so instead filled up a mug of punch and chucked it down his neck. If there was ever a time to drink himself into oblivion it was now. *Am I really that insignificant to her?* They danced their merry dance like there was no one else in the room. He thought back to when he first saw her dancing in a London night club; it felt like yesterday but it was nearly 40 years ago. *I have never looked at another woman since and you have the nerve to do this, in front of me!* He drank and drank and drank. He wasn't sure exactly how long it took for the room to become a TARDIS but he was certain he was ready to throw up. There was no way he would give Ross the satisfaction of seeing that happen, though. Instead he would do what any self-respecting loser would do in his position: go to the toilet, blow chunks and cry ocean-sized tears of resentment and self-loathing.

He somehow managed to get himself upstairs. Either his vision was blurred or the queue for the toilet was a mile long. Either way, the sensible option was to duck into a bedroom and collapse onto a big posh king-sized bed. He sank into the depths of its feather down duvet. The room was spinning but at least he had some semblance of peace, being rid of the misery downstairs. He lay – alone in the pitch black – his clothes wet through but too wasted to care. The urge to vomit had momentarily abated but Five took out his paper bag just in case. As he spread himself out across the bed he felt something resembling a hand touch his thigh. *Is there someone else on the bed?* He reached over to feel who or what it was and found himself cupping a woman's firm, exposed breast. It had been a while but it was definitely a breast. He found himself holding onto it until a moment of awareness washed over him. *Shit, shit.*

'I'm sorry I didn't mean to—'

A slow sensuous moan came back at him through the darkness, 'Oooh.'

His pulse skyrocketed. *What kind of party is this? I should get my head together and go back downstairs.* The temptation, though, like a magnet drew him in. Who was this mysterious woman? Would it be so horribly wrong to have just one kiss? Could anyone blame him for seeking a morsel of human connection, having been starved of it for so long? He slowly lent over and kissed her – a long deep passionate kiss from the plumpest of lips. He could barely remember a kiss like this; it was a profound wonder to behold.

The woman made another groaning noise, 'Ohhhhh.'

That can only be a good sign, can't it? How could something that feels this good be wrong? He was a sexual being after all and he had his needs which were screaming to be met.

'Hi, I'm Five.'

No response.

He lent over and kissed her again, running his hands through her long silky hair. He had felt no greater passion. The fact they were strangers evaporated. They were now two souls sharing a single heartbeat. Vampires sucking the life from one another and promising immortality in return.

'Yeaaaah baby,' came back the honey coated voice, sending sparks up his spine. Her accent had a twang, she definitely wasn't an Essex girl. American maybe? A last flickering doubt entered his mind. *Should I just go back downstairs?* No. For there was a longing in him, that was burning brighter than he'd ever known. He was Eros the god of love and this desire transcended all human concerns.

'Stick it to me big boy,' whispered his secret lover.

Five's combats were round his ankles in a nanosecond and they began a wild wanton desperate love making that only two strangers in a darkened room could have. The intrigue and danger were all part of the tryst of this forbidden love. The duvet flapped like a dragon's wings as Five unleashed the raw power of his sexual energy. It was as if the heavens had opened up to bear witness to the miracle of his performance.

'Keep going baby,' came the panting voice from the darkness.

Five was planning on doing exactly as he was told. Though, after a further three whole minutes of sustained nirvana, just as he was reaching a fierce crescendo, the bedroom light came on and Tina and Ross appeared in door way.

'What the fuck is going on in here?'

Five looked down at his lover, to see that – far from being a sex goddess – she was in fact a sex robot. Not a cheap one, but a high-end silicone love-droid with moving parts and facial expressions.

'Don't you think that's a bit sad mate?'

'I thought she was a woman!'

'And that makes it alright?'

'You've been… almost doing… dirty dancing with him.' Five pointed an accusing finger in Ross's direction.

'What's up with your voice?

'I'm perfectly happy in my voices thanks you.'

'You never normally get *this* drunk.'

'Kiss me lover boy,' said the robot.

'Is that a tampon hanging out of your arse?' asked Ross.

'Pete put it in there.'

'This just gets better and better.' Ross had an ecstatic glint in his eyes.

Candice came swanning into the room holding a Martini Bianco.

'Babe, have you just knobbed our mascot, Mystery? Lance got her cheap, she's got dodgy wiring, you could've fried yourself.'

Arriving next into Five's blurred field of vision was the gothic monstrosity also known as the Count, giggling manically under his crimped fringe, 'Huh, huh.'

'Tina… so you know… it's not sheating… technically… she's non-humanoid.'

'This is exactly what I've been speaking about,' said Tina, 'you're not emotionally mature enough to have an adult relationship. Doing my therapy training has really helped me see who you are.'

'Sex therapy you mean… has it helped you stick your tits into Ross's faces too?'

'Come on,' Tina grabbed Ross by the hand. 'Let's go.'

'Where are you going?'

'We're off to another party, pull your trousers up for fuck's sake,' said Tina.

'How wonderful for you boths.'

The Count snapped a picture with his phone before Five could get his combats back up the right way.

'You're awesome baby,' said Mystery.

'How do I turn her off? asked Five.

'I think you've already done that yeah?' Candice lit up the room with her gargantuan smile while buttoning up Mystery's blouse. 'She can be programmed to send you saucy texts if you'd like me to set it up?'

Ross, having restrained himself far too long already, could not contain himself a second longer. 'Hey Five, I'm dying to ask...'

'Whut?'

'Are friends electric?'

'Huh huh.'

6

A CRIME SCENE

2nd November, 6 a.m.

Something resembling a swamp monster groaned from the darkest depths of the eiderdown. Having been in no state to remove its eyeliner, congealed gunk had fused its eyelashes together, forcing it to ever-so-delicately prize them apart. Its lashing furnace of a brain was blackening the inside of its skull, making the thought of death a most welcome respite. When vision had been partially restored, the duvet rippled as the creature roused itself. A hand reached up for the window sill to lever its torso upright. It creaked and cursed, snarled and spat until, eventually, it achieved its aim. It was at this point the trouble really started.

The bed morphed into a magic roundabout, revolving in a psychedelic blur. Purple swirls from the carpet pirouetted upwards and stuck to the ceiling. Scraping could be heard on the outside of the window. The beast peeled back the curtains to see that the cranes had grown tentacles which were worming their way in through the cracks in the walls. It had to find a way to escape. It could launch itself towards the door and maybe reach it, but what if it failed? The tentacles were now slithering across the floor, squirming their way up the bed posts and leaving a weird green substance in their wake. A giant black pulsating eye appeared at the window, scanning the room for its victim. A jump was

attempted but it was futile, the cranes' tentacles had wound tightly around its legs, causing it to fall face-first into the gurgling green liquid.

Six hours later Five awoke feeling marginally more capable of navigating reality. Luckily, the tentacles had left the building. He closed the curtains tight just to make sure. He moved like a zombie along the hall to the kitchen, splashed cold water onto his face and flicked the kettle on, just as the cuckoo clock chimed for midday. *Shit!* He hurried up the stairs to find Frank sat up in bed, sucking on a cough sweet and thoroughly engrossed in the autobiography of Stevie Nicks. The room was a sauna, the air a fog of manky socks and man sweat. Bile began crawling its way up Five's oesophagus, but before he could be sick he had collapsed on his dad's bed.

'She's left me Dad... I told you she would.'

'I'm sorry son.' Frank swept his sweat-encrusted fringe off his forehead and wrapped his arms around him.

'I can't survive without her.'

'You weren't doing great with her, if I'm being honest.'

'It was 40 years...' His voice trembled.

'It hasn't always been easy between your mother and me you know. Back in the 60s I used to have the groupies hanging off me. She used to get the right hump.'

Five ripped a handful of tissues from the bedside cabinet and rubbed them across his mushy face.

Mags hobbled into the room with the aid of her trusted walking stick and sat down next to her son.

'What's going on love?'

'She's gone off with that bastard Ross.'

'What a bitch.'

'She went off to a party with him and left me behind.'

'You might be reading too much into it, son.'

'I know… I'm right.' Feeling nauseous again Five closed his eyes and lay his head on his mum's lap. He could still hear their laughter rupture inside him like an abscess in his soul. The story would be all over town by now, in every cafe, bookie's, pub and Facebook update. This kind of news travelled fast in Romford and it was generally received like a comedic dream. For Five it was more like a crime scene.

'What am I going to do?' Five bit down on his bottom lip as he held back the tears.

Mags reached over and pulled Five's hand away from the raw crease of his arm. 'One day at a time love, that's all you can do.'

'We'd been having a rocky patch but all relationships have them, don't they?'

'She'll get tired of him,' said Mags. 'No one needs to be six foot five.'

'What's that got to do with anything?'

'Just saying love.'

Sensing a presence, Five looked up to see Don hovering above him. His head obscured the hallway light giving him a glowing yellow aura like the Ready Brek advert from 1980s. Don gave him his 'half smile of the Buddha' which was reserved for spiritual emergencies like these.

'Shall we go for a walk?'

A gap in the rain allowed a ray of winter sun to glisten off the freshly-washed paving stones. The brothers' shadows contorted before them as they stomped through the murky puddles decorating each other with oily mud spots. The growl of relentless construction jerked and jarred in competition with the traffic and people hurrying past gabbling into mobile phones.

'Whatever happened to her? She used to be as unhappy as me once.'

Don put his arm around him.

'She's been saying she's going through a spiritual phase, whatever that means.'

'People change.' Don closed his eyes briefly to reflect on the profundity of those two words.

'I don't' – Five dropped his head – 'I don't know how.'

'This may be the shift you need.'

'What the hell are we going to do without a bass player?'

'Mum can do Tina's bass parts.'

'On her keyboard?'

'At least it will be in time. I was thinking of putting her through an effects pedal.'

'I've got some great news about the judges.' Five raised his eyebrows. 'Pete shagged one of them and the other is my old geography teacher.'

'Shit pits?'

Five nodded and then dipped his chin to his chest.

'He's not going to recognise you after 35 years, you don't even have the same name.'

'Let's hope not.'

Don slowed and propped himself against the arm of a bench. 'Need a breather.'

'We're going to get that pacemaker looked at.' Five took off his scarf and dried a spot for Don to sit down.

'I'm alright, just… unfit.'

'I don't know what I'd do without you.'

'I'm not going anywhere.' Don took a deep breath in.

'No matter what shit happens, we're gonna win this tournament. Imagine supporting Numan, it's what we've always wanted isn't it?'

'That would be great, but remember it's about the music, not the winning.'

Five hopped up onto the bench and stared out over the Saturday crowds flooding out from Romford train station.

'I want to stand on stage in front of thousands of Numanoids and yell, 'We are the Romford Bombers and you… are about to be blown away,' Five's voice cracked.

Don jerked his neck round to look up at him. Thick tears poured down his face.

FIVE'S DIARY

<u>3rd November</u>

<u>4 am</u>

And then there was this.

Of course this.

A repeating history.

Another kick in the guts.

How many can you take before you stop getting back up?

I may never leave this room again.

Just stay in bed, curl up and die.

Let the maggots fight over the tastiest bits of my eyeballs and brain as I slowly decompose into this shitty old mattress. When Ross comes over from the undertaker's, I'd make him give me a tree burial – an oak – so I could grow back, fierce and proud. Knowing that bastard, though, he'd probably then come back with a chainsaw and cut me down. My only wish is that he would then use me for firewood. I'd be reborn again, this time as an ember floating up from the flames. I'd land on his hearth rug, set fire to it and burn his fucking house down.

7 am

The truth is I would never kill myself, that's far too easy. My route will be a subtle but profound alternative. I will simply decline the invitation of life. Spurn the option of existence by dissolving into a bardo realm. I'm sure Don can show me how. It will be a protest against the tyranny of living, the abuse of consciousness. What a lasting message that would send. I'll be a martyr for the undead. I think Pete would be proud of me (I'll leave him my record collection.) Tina will say she saw it coming, that it was the consequence of me never having grown up and taken responsibility for myself. What about taking responsibility for everybody else? Not that I care what she thinks anymore. I would haunt the hell out of Ross. Anyway even if death does come early for me, I'm not scared of it. Know why? Can it really be any worse than living in Romford? Maybe I should move in with Jenny next door and team up on the curtain twitching and eyeballing of strangers. That's the inevitable conclusion of where life leads us isn't it? Incontinence and insanity. That reminds me, I better get dad up.

11 am

Note to self – If you ever read this back, I was talking shit. I can't die, who would look after everyone? And what about the band? That's the only thing that matters now. Soon as we win, everything will be fine again I just know it.

4 pm

I've been thinking, in a way there was a kind of liberation in last night. Being humiliated like that in front of everyone was one of my biggest fears. What is there left to lose? Tina I suppose. I don't care about her anymore though. Why would I want to be with someone who treats me like that? I'm not even going to think about her anymore. She doesn't deserve the airtime. This is just going to focus me even further on winning battle of the bands. She's done me a favour.

6 pm

Tina used to say I just need to accept what happened to me, she was like a broken record with it. Like it was that easy. She must have been absent the day they handed out compassion. She has no idea what it's like to feel completely out of control. To feel like there's a hole inside you that just keeps getting bigger and bigger. I've got that therapy appointment tomorrow. That might be worse than death. Pete reckons I should say 'no comment' to all their questions. He said 'Once they're in your head you've lost your authenticity.' I don't really know what that means but I'm pretty sure he needs therapy more than me. I wish I could talk about what happened but I can barely bring myself to think about it.

7.30 pm

I've just reread the R&DGNFC's official rules governing the Battle of the Numan Tribute Bands. That's an hour I'll never get back. I can't believe there is no policy about judges and/or fan club officials accepting gifts and gratuities. It's insane. What other official body would get away with that? They're probably getting all kinds of back handers. Is it any wonder they're going into liquidation? I've heard all kinds of rumours about how dodgy Candice's husband Lance is. A few years back a whistle-blower came forward. She was an ex-bookkeeper who claimed they were funnelling 30% of their T-shirt sales through an account on the Isle of Man which was funding their winter holidays to Spain. Talk about absolute power corrupting. Also why would they employ non-Numanoid judges to decide who the ultimate Numan tribute act is? It doesn't make any sense. Candice reckons it makes them impartial but how can they pick up on the nuances? I wouldn't ever say this to anyone but I think I embody Numan's essence. It's a spiritual thing (actually that does make me sound like a twat.) I suppose what I really mean is, I've got pedigree. I've been doing this since 1979. I've bought every album the day it was released, been to every tour and I've sung his songs every day for 40 years. And the best bit? Electricity still runs through my veins at exactly the same intensity as it ever did. I always remember going to see him on the Skin Mechanic tour, it was the 25th October, 1989 at the Hammersmith Odeon, I loved that venue. Tina and me got so dressed up that night, I'd just put a red stripe in my hair like Gary used to have in the *Telekon* days. We were skint even by our standards so I raided Dad's spare change jar and just dumped a load of change in my jean pocket. As we stood at the bar ordering our halves of cider (last of the big spenders) the lining in my pocket went and the change went tumbling down my leg and all over the floor. Tina turned around to see me scrambling on all fours picking up loads of 2p pieces. Everyone was laughing at me (I should have spotted a theme developing then!) My point is I humiliated myself just to get a drink so I could enjoy the gig more. I didn't care if people took the piss (Tina did) it's that kind of commitment to the cause that other tribute acts could only dream of and it would be totally lost on those judges. Ross's favourite Numan album is *Machine + Soul.* I rest my case.

8.30 pm

I've just had Stubber on the phone, he's beside himself.

Rambo's been throwing up again. I don't know why he calls me, he thinks because I'm a carer I can give out medical advice. He's been feeding him these big steaks to build his energy up but I'm really not sure that's right. Chihuahuas are supposed to have delicate constitutions aren't they?

7

THE ONLY WAY IS THERAPY

4th of November

The office must have been at best two metres square; it managed to house a desk, a bookshelf and two chairs. Cosy wasn't the word. This was as good as it got for the therapy service, though. NHS budgets don't stretch far and this was just another poorly converted room with a nylon carpet and tatty office furniture.

Mrs Summerisle was dressed in a tight-fitting beige suit that blended nicely with the magnolia walls. Her hair was long and unreasonably frizzy, which had compelled her to wage a war to control it, using an army of hair grips. She had not emerged victorious.

'Good Afternoon Mr Watts—'

'Just call me Five,' he said sitting down in his coat. He wasn't planning on staying long. After lying awake most of the night, he had decided to implement a war-like strategy himself: Operation Give Nothing Away and Get Out Alive.

'You can call me Judy.'

Five nodded, crossed his arms and tried to tuck his feet under his chair to stop them from getting too close to her. The heat was unbearable.

'I'm afraid the radiators are set at the same temperatures for the big and small rooms. I thought we were trying to save money.' She smiled and reached behind her to yank the window open. A blackbird was sat on the ledge looking in, cocking its head from side to side as if it had taken a personal interest in Five's affairs.

'That's quite a unique name.'

'What's wrong with that?'

'Nothing.' Judy opened a large black folder and flicked through an official looking document. 'You had a carer's assessment which highlighted some issues that Doctor Ewan felt would be helpful for you to look at. Is that correct?'

After the faintest of reluctant nods, Five looked up to notice a muscle that spasmed in the corner of Judy's eye.

Did she wink at me?

It happened again.

Don't stare.

'Maybe we could start with a short, potted history? Were you born in Romford?'

'No... I don't know. I was left in a cot at the entrance of Romford A & E, I was only six months old. There was no trace of my real parents.'

'How have things been with your adopted family?'

'They're my whole world. They have always supported me growing up. The irony is, I care for *all* of them now.'

'Did you need a lot of support?'

'I always felt different... a bit alien... maybe that's what being adopted feels like.'

I'm giving away too much.

Judy motioned to speak but paused and they sat in silence. The second hand of a dated office clock clicked clumsily as it navigated its way towards the future. Five's diaphragm tightened.

'How do you manage in your caring role?'

'I get so tired. I worry I'm not doing a good enough job… I worry about them too much probably.'

'Would you like to say a bit more about that?'

'My younger brother, Don, had a by-pass op last year and they fitted a pacemaker. He's not been right since. Doctor says he has to take it easy. Luckily he does tons of meditation.' Five paused to make eye contact with Judy. 'He's very spiritual, he's been to India… I think he might be enlightened.'

Judy smiled and raised her eyebrows as high as she could without overdoing it.

'Thing is, the family are all musical and we play in a band together, a Gary Numan tribute act. Don plays guitar and I worry it might be too much for him.'

The blackbird sidestepped along the window ledge to get a better view of Five. Looking as though it had found its optimum vantage point, it stopped and nestled into itself.

'Music can be very therapeutic; do you play many concerts?'

'Our main event is the battle of the Numan tribute bands in London every December. They have acts from all over the world. We have won every year apart from last year when this new band came first.' Five ground his teeth and chewed on an outcrop of flesh on the inside of his cheek.

'Did you find it difficult to lose?'

'Their lead singer… is a real gloating bastard. He'll do anything to get one over on me. Even…'

'Yes?'

'Go off with my girlfriend… Tina.' The edges of his mouth quivered.

'I'm sorry to hear that.'

'We'd been together nearly forty years.'

'Would you like to say more about that?' Julie repositioned a hair grip to keep her fringe from invading her forehead.

'I… can't.' Five's attention was taken by the walls that seemed to moving slowly towards him. The blackbird jerked its head forward and squinted, looking like it was growing impatient with the proceedings.

Julie flicked through the pages of Five's file, pausing to read a passage. A bead of sweat popped out from Five's temple and trickled down the side of his face.

'You said in your assessment you have been suffering from quite severe panic attacks for the last year?'

Why did I say that?

'I'm fine, I just need a few early nights to get back on track.'

'You said it was triggered by an event?'

Five fell mute.

There's no way I'm telling you that.

He took a sharp in-breath. 'Don't we all have something we wish hadn't happened?'

'Perhaps.'

The words hung uneasily in the air between them. Five looked down and realised his legs were slowly shrinking. The arm rests of his chair were rising up and enclosing him like the sides of a coffin. *I can't die like this, what would my epitaph be? "Here lies Five, a man so inconsequential he evaporated."*

He grabbed at the familiar crease in his arm and squeezed as if to strangle it.

I can't breathe.

Wink, wink.

Don't stare.

Judy tweaked her hair grip.

Stop fucking doing that.

CLICK, CLICK, CLICK.

Is that clock getting louder?

All the while, the blackbird's beady eyes burrowed into his unveiled soul.

Judy was getting taller. Her head was almost touching the ceiling. It was just Five's luck to get the world's tallest therapist.

And if that wasn't bad enough, the walls now seemed to emit a low rumble as every one of their bricks tiptoed toward him, shrinking the room inch by inch, breath by tortured breath.

I'm gonna have to run for it.

Five had at last found his superpower, he had become the incredible shrinking man.

I feel like I'm two inches tall.

Judy peered down from the ceiling. 'Are you OK?' Her words echoed round the room, so loudly they were almost ear-splitting. 'You look a little pale.'

He pulled his brown paper bag out of his back pocket and breathed into it, hard and long.

'Would you like some water?'

He took the glass and glugged it back like he'd been lost in the Sahara.

Judy slowly morphed back to her normal size.

'You'll have to excuse me… I've just been letting things get to me lately.'

'Would you like me to go through some exercises with you to help with anxiety?'

'My brother has taught me all the calming exercises under the sun, but they don't seem to work.'

'Do you do them?'

'No... Look, I don't want to be rude but I don't need your help. We're gonna win the competition again this year and everything will be fine.'

Judy didn't reply, flicking through the pages of his assessment without stopping to read anything.

Five uncrossed his arms.

'Shall we meet the same time next week?'

'I don't need to come again, do I?'

'That's down to you. Why don't you go home and reflect on today and get in touch if you think it would be helpful to see me again. Does that sound fair?'

'Yeah.'

The blackbird flicked his head as if unimpressed with the day's offering and hopped off the window ledge.

'Do you keep a diary?'

'Since I was 15.'

Maybe we could look at it together next time?'

Five gave another micro nod as he got up and headed towards the door, still clutching his arm.

Never in a billion years.

8

REMEMBER, REMEMBER

5th November

When you're an international hacker – worming your way into the most guarded secrets in the corridors of power – you must be a virtual ninja. As untraceable as a grain of sand in a tsunami and leaving not a single whisper you ever existed. On this most auspicious of days, the boys had hunted out at a new clandestine and largely unmonitored location. Romford library. Reference section.

Drafts circled the ceiling rose of the dilapidated Edwardian building like sharks in a whirlpool. Everything about the place was like stepping back in time. Five ran his index finger along the top of a row of encyclopaedias, unleashing reams of dust into the dank surroundings. The only allowable impingement upon the building's noble silence was from the head librarian operating an antiquated photocopy machine that droned away in the background. In the centre of the room, a mandala of fluorescent strip lights hung down in precise equidistant lines illuminating the reading area, a large mahogany table where a rather morose-looking individual with a head like a wilting pumpkin sat submerged in a copy of the day's *Financial Times*.

Pete ripped off his pollution mask, slammed down his rucksack and grunted as he collapsed at the table – an act of hostility that was met with a host of tuts, sighs and minor bodily adjustments; the kind that older British people use to register their dissatisfaction. Pete replied with a grin that exposed a fine crop of yellow, furry teeth.

The pumpkin peered over the top of his newspaper, suspiciously eyeballing the depraved hoodlums who dared enter this most precious of inner sanctums.

Five nuzzled up close to Pete as he flapped open his laptop, its start-up tune causing further bodily adjustments, that Pete was utterly oblivious to. When you are tasked with delivering world peace it's all about keeping your focus. When that screen was lit up it only meant one thing, Zebedee Mind Love was open for business.

'There is a computer section downstairs, you know,' muttered the pumpkin.

'Ignore that old tosser,' said Pete in his gravelly monotone whilst nudging Five playfully in the ribs.

Wrestling his notepad out of his combats, Five narrowed his eyes and jotted down a message:

Don't get us kicked out! Let's write the hacking-related stuff down in here, it will just look like we are studying together.

Pete nodded.

Found out anything?

Pete shrugged and picked up the pen:

I can't find a profile for Ross anywhere, no personal social media, no band account, nothing.

Bit odd isn't it? Five screwed up his face.

Pete replied: But not do I.

My point exactly.

'Touché brother!' Pete blurted before exploding into a machine gun cackle.

'Can you please be quiet?' a voice arose from the darkest depths of the *Financial Times*.

Pete pointed back to the notepad.

There's one possibility we definitely shouldn't rule out.

What?

They could be from another dimension.

How Pete could write that and look so earnest was a miracle. Five sniggered, grabbed the pen and, cocking his right eyebrow:

As long as we also don't rule out that you're the world's biggest space cadet?

Pete gave him a kiss on the cheek and whispered, 'You love it, you tart,' in his ear.

Something's not right about Ross though, he didn't even know Tubeway Army started off as a guitar band, tell me that's not strange?

Even Stubber knows that. Wrote Pete.

Steady.

Pete scribbled fiercely:

It gets weirder, last night I hacked the NHS database and found a medical record for a Mr Ross Patterson, 45 years old, 6 foot 5, blue hair. It's definitely him.

Pete brought up the document on his laptop.

He had a check-up last month and he was given a clean bill of health.

The lying bastard. I've got to try to warn Tina.

Displaying his multi-tasking skills, Pete excavated the contents of his nose with one hand whilst clicking frantically on his mouse between multiple websites with the other.

The pumpkin lowered his paper and growled through nicotine-stained teeth.

Pete puckered his lips and blew him a kiss, causing the paper drawbridge to be rapidly hoisted upwards.

'Stop it,' whispered Five, 'You'll get us thrown out.'

Pete wrote another message:

Fear not brother, I've programmed a bot to trawl the dark web. If there's anything to find, I'll find it.

One of the tabs already open on Pete's browser was his dating profile. Five pulled the laptop towards him and gawped at the screen.

'How's the dating going?' he whispered.

'Fucking dire brother.' Pete was unaware he had raised his voice again. 'I haven't had a bunk up for weeks.'

'Can you keep your romantic life to yourself, please?' said the pumpkin, whose right eye was beginning to bulge.

'There's nothing romantic about it, mate,' replied Pete, raising his voice further. 'The problem is you haven't got a clue who's gonna turn up. This guy wrote to me last week, he looked like a bronzed Adonis in his photo. The bloke who actually turned up had a complexion like a bagman's ballbag. You should be able to do 'em on the Trade Descriptions Act. What's wrong with embracing your wrinkles?'

'I'm trying to embrace current affairs,' said the pumpkin, scanning the library for somewhere else to sit.

Five kicked Pete's leg under the table. 'The librarian's looking over at us.'

'Trust me brother, online dating is a lesson in self-harm, you're best avoiding it.'

Five could feel his palms growing increasingly clammy as he clicked away on Pete's mouse. He stared at his dating profile with a blend of fascination and mild nausea. *How would I even find the confidence to do something like this?*

'I've just updated my tag-line to spell out exactly what I'm looking for.'

Five read it out. 'Pan-sexual Non-Binary Gender Anarchist Searching for Non-monogamous Polyamory.'

'It's important to be clear,' said Pete.

'At least you're getting out and meeting people.'

'It's all disco dollies in this town though, what's the point?'

'Have you tried speed dating?'

'Nah, I've tried dating on speed though. I met this woman for coffee, she could have bored the tits off a zombie. I escaped to the bogs for a few lines, and then I told her about all the impending reptilian invasion. She paid the bill and left. It was my best date so far.'

'This is intolerable,' spat the pumpkin, just loud enough to alert the attention of the librarian again who looked up from her data entry as if her brain had stopped working.

Five rubbed at his arm.

'I thought we had free speech in this country,' Pete belted out. 'I'm exercising my human right to—'

'Yes but does it really need to be done in a library?' Both the pumpkin's eyes were bulging now.

'Piss off grandad, just 'cos you're not getting any.'

'I am, actually.'

Pete looked stunned and more than a little unsure as to how to respond.

'Er… really?'

'My wife and I have an extremely robust love life if you must know.'

'I just thought—'

'Because I'm old?'

'Well… er…'

'I dread to imagine what kind of perverted swamp monster would agree to sleep with you.'

'I can't believe this,' said Pete. At that moment the librarian approached the table and put her hand on Pete's shoulder.

'I think you should leave now sir.'

'It's him you should be throwing out,' Pete waggled his finger accusingly at his bulbous nemesis.

Five picked up Pete's laptop and stood up. 'Let's go mate.'

Pete, however, had other ideas and stayed rooted to his seat to continue the challenge.

'I shouldn't have to leave, it's my human right not to have to put up with this abuse.'

'What you going do about it?' asked the pumpkin.

Again, unsure what to say, Pete spluttered, 'I'll... call the police.'

'I thought you were anarchist?'

'I'm a prisoner in a corrupt system, what choice do I have?

'So you're not *really* an anarchist?'

'I fucking am.'

The librarian decided to join in. It was probably the only excitement the place had seen in weeks. 'I bet you're on Jobseeker's, aren't you?'

Pete pretended there was something important on his phone he had to attend to so he could avoid answering.

She wasn't giving up easily either, though, and pushed him further, 'Where do you live then?'

'In an off-grid, intentional, eco-dwelling—'

'Where?'

Pete's shoulders dropped, 'In my mum's back garden.'

'Aha!' The pumpkin's eyes lit up as he spotted his opportunity. 'We have the reincarnation of Guy Fawkes before us, and today of all days!'

The librarian broke out in a rapturous applause, making much more noise than Pete ever had.

The pumpkin stood up to adopt a Shakespearian pose. He cleared his throat and recited from an imaginary text before him, 'Remember, remember, the fifth of November, the gunpowder, treason and plot...'

Five yanked on Pete's arm. 'Right that's it, we're going NOW!' He marched off towards the exit, hoping Pete would follow him. The scream from the librarian however was a fairly good indication that Pete had not. Instead he had decided to climb up onto the mahogany table and drop his trousers. The strip lights refracted off his goose pimpled back-side as he danced around the table kicking books and news-papers into the air.

'You wanna see some fucking anarchy?'

The librarian sprinted like a wildebeest for the security guard whilst the pumpkin rolled his sleeves back in prepara-tion for fisticuffs.

For the grand finale of the performance, Pete removed his jeans completely and then raised his arms to perform a series of pirouettes across the table. His turning technique was exemplary, and, after a successful first turn, he looked like he was contemplating going for the double. Though he hated being seen as pretentious and opted for an "en pointe" pushing himself upward onto the tips of his DM's. He was anything but a philistine. The overall performance was an extremely bold choice of disparate forms, reminiscent of surrealist street art or, even, early Dada. Though, like all great works of the avant-garde, they are rarely recognised at the time and it would have been futile of Pete to expect any welcome for an encore. Instead, an alarm sounded and hordes of perplexed looking individuals came flooding out from the book aisles and headed for the exit.

Luckily, Five managed to get Pete's trousers back on and drag him from the building before the police arrived.

9

SWIPE LEFT

25th November

Wanted

One-legged goth/emo with a size 9 foot needed to go halfsies on some men's vegan buckle boots.
N.B. I need the right foot.

'What do you reckon?' said Five, reading out his advert in the *Friday Ad*.

'Bit of a long shot ain't it?' said Mags.

'He's not wearing that bloody slipper onstage.'

'Stubber said he's got an old cowboy boot he can use.'

'That's worse.'

'What about one of his old tennis shoes? They're not seeing much action.'

'Not happening. We've got to be *on* it this year. The stakes have never been higher and that means every detail has to be right.'

Mags nodded intently, trying her best to look like she was with the program. 'Speak of the devil.'

Worried he might be late, Frank came whizzing into the kitchen and took his place at the table. A pan of almond milk bubbled on the stove in preparation for the evening's hot chocolate and crumpets. It was 8pm. Five's routine exhaustion had crept out of the ether and cocooned him like a wet rag.

Stubber had just been round and, having been egged on by Frank, he thought it would be hysterical to download a dating app onto Five's phone when he was out of the room. It had been over 40 years since he was in the shop window and things were different then. Dating in the 1970s was a tricky bit of business for a beta male. There was no social media or dating apps to seek out your dream date. In those days when someone caught your fancy, you had to resort to radical means. Look them straight in the eyes and talk to them. It was terrifying. It's a wonder the British population ever survived. Thank god for alcohol. It was all so easy now, you just swipe left for no and right for yes, even robots could do it. Let's hope for Five's sake they weren't.

With Mags and Frank blowing into their steamy mugs, Five collapsed at the table next to them and massaged his temples with deep circular finger rotations. He'd been averaging about three hours sleep a night since the party and rarely got a moment to himself.

'You gonna give it a go then?' asked Frank

Five put his glasses on, opened up the app and stared at it in a blurry stupor. He was at best conflicted about fast technology – how it was colonizing our lives. That said, he had caught himself staring at old ladies' legs on the bus on the way to Sainsbury's this morning. Maybe now was the time to act. *Why shouldn't I? Tina isn't the only one who can chuck it about. I'm the lead singer of a rock band, that's gotta count for something, hasn't it?* He uploaded a photo of himself onstage from two years ago. Though it could have been 5 years ago. *Who's gonna know?* The next step was to write something interesting about himself. This he could do.

Lead singer of the world's leading Gary Numan tribute band. Soon to be supporting Numan at the Royal Albert Hall in January. I'm an outsider, a square peg, a maverick, unapologetically alternative. Hobbies include: song writing, paragliding and vegan cooking. You? If you feel like something's always about to go wrong, I'm sure we'll get along.

'Come on then' – Frank doubled over to get a look at the screen – 'let's see what the talent's like.'

Five tapped the search button and first up was a professional looking woman from Barking.

'She looks too old for you.'

'She's 45, Dad.'

'Her best days are behind her by the looks of it.'

'Is that what you say about me when I'm not in the room?' said Mags.

'Your beauty is timeless my darlin'.'

Swipe left.

'What's with the bunny ears?'

'You've got to look beyond that,' said Mags

'I can't.'

Swipe left.

'I would,' said Frank, blowing his nose.

'Your knee would give way,' said Mags

'I'd give it a bloody good go.'

'That's a definite no then.'

Swipe left.

'Why is she stood next to a guy that looks like Brad Pitt?' asked Mags.

'That is Brad Pitt,' said Five.

Swipe left.

'She's miles away, I can't see her face.'

Swipe left.

'You've got to give 'em a chance, son.'

'Why is she wearing dark glasses indoors?'

'It's fashion,' said Mags.

'It's November in Romford.'

Swipe left.

'She's pretty,' said Frank.

'She's using one of those face filters.'

'What's that?'

'It makes someone who's 50 look 18 again.'

'Can you get me one?' asked Mags.

'Why can't people just be who they are?'

Swipe left.

'You wear makeup, son.'

'That's different, I'm an artist.'

'Have you got a photo where you're not wearing that baseball cap?'

'My hair's a mess.'

'Why don't you get a new syrup?'

'How many times have I got to tell you? – it's a weave.'

'I'd feel weird having plastic hair on my barnet,' said Mags.

'It's human hair, I get it online from China.'

'It's probably from the dissidents,' said Frank, nodding to himself with a hot chocolate moustache.

'What?'

'They shave the heads of political prisoners before locking them up, don't they?'

'How do you know?'

'I saw it on YourTube. Whoever sweeps up has got 'emselves a nice little side-line I reckon.' Frank rubbed his thumb and index finger together.

Five massaged the back of his neck, unsure whether to laugh or cry, 'I can't afford a refit at the moment... unless you're both happy to go without puddings for a few weeks?'

The response was as if a tumbleweed had swept across the kitchen table.

'They all seem to have photos hiking up the Himalayas.'

Swipe left.

'I should use that one of me in Dagenham park.'

'It's not quite as exotic, love.'

'No, it's more dangerous though.' Five bit into a cold crumpet. 'I'm never gonna meet someone like this.'

'Whatever happened to seeing someone you like in the street and asking them out on a date?' asked Frank.

'I think it's illegal now,' said Mags.

Five's shoulders bobbed up and down as he tried to stifle his laughter. 'This is the age of disposable romances, commitment is a thing of the past. As soon as you grow weary of someone you just tap a button and a machine does your dirty work for you. No one takes responsibility anymore, people just run screaming from one relationship to the next.'

'That's deep love.'

Swipe left.

'You'll meet someone at a gig once we're playing more regularly again,' said Frank, picking bits of crumpet out of his beard.

'I think you're right dad.'

Swipe left.

'If Tina had shown up on something like this who's to say I would have chosen her? Why do we now think it's OK to let an algorithm shape our destiny? Me and Don are writing a song about it, actually, called 'The Clones.''

'We look forward to hearing that.' Frank elbowed Mags.

'I read about a guy who got married to a sex robot,' said Mags

Five scanned her face. *Has someone said something to her?* 'You can get robot carers too. Maybe we should try one?'

Tumbleweed swept across the kitchen table once again.

Swipe left.

'This is depressing.'

Swipe left.

'I think… I'm gonna give this up as a bad idea.'

The next profile that came up was a 45-year-old lady with green hair wearing a Nine Inch Nails T-shirt. Her tagline was, 'An American Werewolf in London.'

Swipe right.

A WARNING

Five

Watch out for Ross, he's not sick, he's playing you 22:51

Tina

What?? 23:01

Five

He's not really sick 23:02

Tina

You need to cut this out mate, it's gonna make you sick 23:03

Five

Don't say I didn't warn you. 23:05

Tina

I hope the counselling is helping X 23:06

10

BARBECUED SUSHI

25th November

Over at the undertaker's, Ross had called to invite Tina to join him on his lunch break. To be completely accurate, he had texted her to say *'I'm too busy to get out! You couldn't bring a burger over could you? PS bit skint too, can I owe you?'* This was romance Romford style, everything the modern woman could desire: the wooing, the adoration, the autonomy of financial responsibility and a bit of nosebag with the recently departed. Truth be known Tina herself was a bit skint. She had just spent her week's food allowance on sushi as a surprise for Ross. He told her he couldn't get enough of it so she was hoping to entice him back to her place before it went off, meaning tonight. She didn't have a clue where she'd find the cash to buy food for the rest of the week. It wasn't as though student loans grew on trees. Well they did, but you have to pay them back. Well you don't, but that's not the point.

Tina swept her hair out of her face and narrowed her gaze

as she looked into Ross's fathoms-deep blue eyes. She laid two large bags of chips down on the coffin lid that was serving as a makeshift table and carefully peeled back the moist paper wrapping. Shuddering as the steam and vinegar lashed at her senses, she moved a bottle of formaldehyde out the way and, leaning in close – not breaking eye contact – she picked up a chip and blew on it before slowly caressing it with the tip of her tongue. She then dipped the chip into a sachet of mayonnaise and smeared it over her bright crimson lips. Ross edged forward and motioned to whisper in her ear. She grabbed his arm to steady herself as though a single word could shatter her into a million ecstasies.

'Did you get any barbecue sauce?'

'Huh?'

'For my burger?'

'Oh ... in my bag.'

Tina winced as she watched him devour his food. It wasn't going to be easy dating a meat eater after being with a vegan for so long. Ross ate like a rabid hyena, only pausing to make self-satisfied moans as he licked the excess sauce off his fingers. With only a single-glazed window, the room was fairly gloomy and had that musty aroma of rising damp. Coffins were stacked high against the wall on the left side of the room and, to her right, were racks upon racks of synthesizers in various states of repair. Below them, a mountain of electrical parts balanced perilously on an old workbench. Tina pointed to a large packing crate in the middle of the room filled with broken up panels and strange looking wires. 'What's all that gear for?'

'I'm making Five a new girlfriend.'

'That's not funny,' said Tina, half concealing a smile.

'It is a bit.'

'Aye a bit.'

Ross got up and strutted over to the crate, placed the lid back on it and picked up a hammer to bang a nail into each corner. He returned to the coffin and flicked up the volume on his radio. He was an avid news listener and would never miss the headlines even though it prompted mood swings of HRT proportions. In much the same way that Five was affected by the weather, Ross responded to reports of crime statistics as though the mayor of Romford had just shined a bat-signal for him.

'*Three more fatal stabbings this week in London…*'

'Things are getting messy out there.' Tina wiped her salty fingers on her jeans. 'Where does all that hate come from?'

'Evil scum that's who.' Ross dumped the remains of his burger down onto the coffin lid. A piece of gherkin fell out onto the bronzed inscription that read '*In honour of Corporal John Hallam - A gentleman and a friend.*'

'Not sure I believe in evil… some people get a rough start is all.' Tina moved round the coffin to get closer to Ross.

'I was thrown in a boarding school when I was seven. A twisted psychopath of a dorm master spent years beating the shit out of me regardless of how I behaved. Does that constitute a rough start?'

Tina wrapped her arm around him.

'I'll never forget his snarling expression as he bent his cane in front of me. No one can tell me that's not evil.'

'That's awful.' She kissed him gently on the cheek. 'How about knocking off early and coming back to my place? I've got a surprise for you.'

'You asked what the parts are for, I make model aeroplanes then send them to an orphanage. I chose to turn my life around and do something positive. Some people are just born bad and someone needs to stand up to them.'

'That's what the law is for, no?' Tina pulled at the neck of her jumper to let some air in.

'There are a lot more dangerous things than psycho teachers to fight in this world you know.'

'What do you mean?'

A flicker of recognition spread across Ross's face. 'Ignore me... I'm getting carried away. Let's talk about you, what do you want to do with your life?'

'I want to make a difference. I promised my dad I'd do something that would make him proud.'

'He's not around anymore?'

'Nae' – Tina paused – 'but he's always with me.'

Ross put his arm around her waist and pulled her towards him. 'My dad always used to say you can judge a person's worth by the contribution they make to society. It was the only thing he ever said that ever made sense to me.'

Tina swept her fingers through his hair. 'So how about my place then?'

'Nah sorry, I've gotta get Mr Hallam up the crematorium.' He took out a tissue and wiped the splattering of barbecue sauce off the coffin lid. 'He's being barbecued today.'

'What about tonight?'

'I've got a deadline to fix one of Numan's synths, he's out on tour next week, if I don't get it done I could lose the contract.'

Tina dropped her head, picked up her phone and stared blankly at it.

Ross pulled out a packet of cigarettes, tapping one out on the edge of the coffin lid. 'Look, if I get this finished in time we can fly out to LA together. You could get to meet Numan.'

'Five would hate me.'

'And?'

'You dinnae stop loving someone you've been with for 40 years overnight. Anyway, should you be flying... being sick n' all?'

'Oh... yeah' – he pulled on his trench coat – 'I forgot to tell you... I'm in remission.'

'You forgot?'

'I've been busy with rehearsals.'

'Too busy to tell me you're not dying?'

'We're all dying Tina. It's just a matter of when.'

'What sort of answer is that?'

Ross pushed the coffin over towards the door. 'I haven't got time for this.'

'I've just spent a small fortune on sushi for you.'

'Why? I can't stand the stuff.'

'But you said you loved it?'

'I was taking the piss.'

'Aye… hilarious.'

Ross shouted over his shoulder as he disappeared out of the door, 'You'll really need to get a sense of humour if this is gonna work.'

Tina gritted her teeth and stared at the empty doorway. 'And you're gonna need a fucking personality.'

DOG AND BONE

Five
Alright Stubsy, a date for the diary, next Thursday the Romford
gazette are over to interview us about the tournament! 09:38

Stubber
Wouldn't miss it for the world mate 09:41

Five
Also was wondering if you knew anywhere we could borrow a
synthesizser? 09:46

Stubber
Won't have time before the gig, but watch this space.
P.S. If Barbara calls, tell her I stayed at yours on Saturday night.
10:49

BOOTY CALL

Mags

Its like bloody Siberia in the front room. 17:49

Frank

COME.UP! ITS.LIKE.THE.MOJAVE.
DESERT.IN HERE 17:58

Mags

On my way! 18:01

Frank

BRING.THE.HOB.NOBS! 18:03

FIVE'S DIARY

26th November

4.30 am

I can't stop worrying about Don. I have this fear his heart could give out at anytime. He reckons I'm worrying about nothing and that meditation will heal him. He's started listening to the sound of humpback whales because he reckons they are the guardians of the planet and give off a healing frequency. If thats true, I wonder who their ombudsman is? They are doing a fucking shit job.

9 am

I got a postcard today. It's got a shiny Mirror surface on the front and the back was blank apart from some printed text that read: 'If you are too scared to tell yourself the truth, try telling it to someone else first.' Who the hell sent that? Pete's got to be a contender.

6.30 pm

Everyone always wants to know where I got my name from. It's really annoying. I refuse to explain it to non-Numanoids though, why do they need to know? And if you are a Numanoid you would know already so I don't need to

95

explain it to anyone. Ross doesn't get it. That should say something. I think you should have to register to become a Numanoid, pass certain tests and maybe even get interviewed by Gary? He's probably too busy though.

27th November

10.15 am

Mum's been winding me up recently, always coming up with new ways to 'fix my life'. There's been Yoga, Tai chi, a health spa, and todays is making sure I do 10,000 steps a day (I'm knackered after 100!) The problem is she gets all her ideas from articles she rips out of the women's magazines she reads at the hairdressers. Magazines that are largely aimed at 18-25 year old women. Thankfully I've hit upon two magic words that can freeze her into submission. 'External Carers'. She goes quiet for a few days then it all starts again.

7 pm

Tina was always going on about the fact I 'haven't grown up,' whatever that means. Just 'cause I don't fit her expectations. I refuse to conform to anyone else's standard of emotional or spiritual development. What gives her the right to dictate to me? Am I supposed to believe there's an objective standard for human development? Did I miss a lecture? Try telling that to hordes of people in this town that hit the pub every weekend, get shit faced and beat the crap out of each other. The fact is, in society's eyes, however fucked up your life is, as long as you've got a job and got a credit card you get to be a grown up. If you walk any other kind of path, people get jealous and accuse you of 'not towing the line.' Just because you're not stuck in the same trap as them. Fuck that. If those are the choices, I'll happily remain adolescent.

28th November

<u>4 pm</u>

I had a chat with Pete on the phone. He's been left some money by an uncle and wants to buy some land to set up an intentional eco community. I've always liked that idea. I'd want one based on Bedouin principles but with Numanoids instead of Bedouins. Pete insists it's got to be an anti-capitalist, anti-ownership, anti-fascist, anti-imperialist, freegan, gender-neutral, polyamorous free love commune (I might have left some terms out there) He wants me to help start it up. I asked him what decision making process it would have and he said he would make all the decisions as the land would be in his name. I told him he's playing god but he got out of it by saying he'd only be in charge temporarily until the reptilian overlords arrive. What can you say to that? Even if these aliens do exist who's to say they are highly evolved? They might be thick as shit. The only people I'd trust in that role is Don or Gary Numan. If either of them is keen on the role of a benevolent world dictator, I'm in. Otherwise forget it. Saying that I think I might sign up just so I can watch Pete explain his vision to the council planning officer.

29th November

<u>6 am</u>

I woke up with purple arms today. I'm sure I'd be warmer sleeping in the garden. I'm thinking of moving into Dad's room it's like a furnace in there. I think it must be all the decomposing socks that make it so hot. It would be good to have a character more like his. He seems to rumble on no matter what's thrown at him. Man can he talk shit though. He never seems happier than when he's waxing lyrical about something he knows absolutely nothing about. I hid his slipper in the loft two days ago. I better get it down.

<u>5pm</u>

What kind of life is this? We keep walking in a straight

line. Hoping everything will pan out. Maybe it does for a while, and we get a bit of confidence. But our whole security is as fragile butterflies in a tornado. Life is a random game of fortune and tragedy. One wrong decision or quirk of nature could send your life spinning off its axis. How can anyone feel secure in that knowledge? The lie we are brought up to believe is that we are in control of our destiny. It's such an alluring idea it's hard not to believe but the fact is, it's a fairy tale. Maybe I think too much? Don always asks me, 'Is it better to be a dissatisfied human being or a satisfied pig?' He never tells me the answer though. Thanks Don.

30th November

5 am

Tina came round to collect some of her stuff this morning. She wouldn't tell me if she was seeing Ross. Does she think I'm stupid? She said she wanted us to stay friends. I told her I'd think about it once I've grown up. I wouldn't care if I never saw her again. I know that sounds harsh but it's how I feel.

AMERICAN WEREWOLVES

1st December

F ive's phone pinged, an unfamiliar ringtone. He was still in bed. Fumbling over the bedside table, he grabbed it and, jabbing in his code, the screen informed him it was 6.30 am. He never got texts this early...

You have a new message from 'American Werewolf in London.'

Hey ;-)

Hi

We matched!

Shit she's online

Yeah!

A tingle ran up Five's spine. A sensation he had forgotten was possible.

I'm Jax

Five

Just play it cool

Great name, I'm over here from the U.S.

Me too

Why the fuck did I say that?

No way! (Wisconsin)

Awesome. (L.A.)

What am I doing? Five felt an itchy sensation in the crease of his arm.

You sing in a Numan tribute band?

Yeah, we're doing a big tour over here.

Are we?

Cool! I've been a Numanoid since forever.

Yeah, same, I'm old school, started the band in 1979

Meet up?

Yeah!

There's this new wild food eatery I wanna check out in Camden?

Sure.

How much is that gonna set me back?

Five jumped out of bed in his pants and, after a little jig about his bedroom, pointed at himself in his dressing table mirror.

'Who's fucking laughing now?'

1 2

PLANET OF THE ELEPHANTS

5th December

F ive thought he'd seen the old woman at the other end of the tube, so he got off early and walked the rest way of the way, cursing the rain. He arrived at the Eat Wild restaurant a few minutes early, giving him enough time to check his reflection in the window. Even though he was utterly drenched, that bit of hair on his crown was still sticking up, no doubt just to spite him. He tried to smear it down with brute force, to no avail. He wondered if the new combat trousers (bought specially for the occasion) made him look too keen – or god forbid – desperate. *What's the big deal? It's just a date.* He checked the time again. She'll be here any second. He could feel his heart beating faster, his stomach churning. *Just be yourself... no don't do that... why did I agree to this?*

'Five?'

He turned around and there she was, just like her photo,

but more attractive. What a relief. 'Hi Jax,' his voice squeaked like an old bicycle. 'Did you get caught in the rain too?'

Jax nodded. 'You have a British accent?'

'Er yeah, I've been touring over here for years and I've got a crash pad in Essex. The accent there is quite alluring so it kind of stuck.' *What? She'll never believe that.*

Jax had the most striking blue eyes; the left was darker than the right. It gave her an otherworldly look. A bit Bowie. If things worked out he could never introduce her to Pete. Or Stubber. Or anyone, for that matter.

They were led to seats by the window. The seating was arranged around a series of densely packed circular tables surrounding the perimeter of the room. Five had to squeeze in tightly behind a man who was devouring a meal large enough to feed a rugby team. The layout was clearly designed to offer everyone a view of the main attraction, a garishly lit fish tank full to the brim with prawns, crabs and a solitary lobster whose purple shell glistened, giving it a two-tone effect. The expression of the creature was quite peculiar. His little black eyes dilated as it rubbed its whiskers up against the tank wall. Five thought it looked suspiciously aware of the fact he would soon be shuffling off this mortal coil. One glance at the laminated menu told Five there would be nothing he could eat here. 'I didn't know this would be a dead flesh restaurant.'

'Is there a problem?'

'I'm vegan.'

'You should have said.'

Five nodded and put down the menu.

'It's got great reviews here, I'm sure they must have something you can eat?'

Five shrugged his shoulders.

'I have a lot of respect for vegans, I agree with it ethically but I love meat *way* too much,' she laughed and swept her fringe back off her forehead.

Five's abdomen contracted. *How many times have I heard that before? It's just lame.*

'I looked you up on Instagram, you sound just like Numan.'

'Thanks.'

'Apart from the keyboards.' She fiddled with her nose-ring.

Five crumpled up his face and picked up the menu again.

'The profile said you are from Roomford.'

'Romford, it's where our studio and rehearsal rooms are.'

'I bet you guys have some crazy parties hey?'

'Yeah… you know how it is.' Five let out a chuckle and flicked his head upwards. *You're in bed by 8pm you dick head.*

The man with the gargantuan feast behind Five was quite possibly the world's noisiest eater – a grunting hog in a track-suit – shovelling food down his gullet like it was an eating competition. Pausing only momentarily to carefully re-tuck his serviette around his neck before diving back into the carnage. Bits of ripped flesh dribbled down his chin as he swigged back huge mouthfuls of red wine. Five's shoulders edged a little closer up towards his ears.

'How are we all doing today?' interjected the waitress as a welcome respite. 'You guys ready to order?'

'Do you have anything to eat that isn't swimming?' asked Five.

'We have some great wild boar dishes.'

'He's a vegan,' said Jax, frowning at the waitress.

It's not a fucking disability.

'So many celebrities are vegan now aren't they?' replied the waitress.

Five smiled, unsure if she had intended to include him on that list.

'I'll have a beer and the lobster please,' said Jax.

'Good choice.' The waitress lent in closer, 'the meat is so tender.'

103

A wave of repulsion reverberated through Five's body. Of all the shit things he had ever heard anyone say, that easily made the top ten.

'There he is!' said the waitress pointing towards the tank, adding brightly, 'wave!'

'Ha ha!' Jaz waved at the forlorn creature.

Five could barely bring himself to look at the beast. Its beady little eyes looked back at him as if he'd spotted a kindred spirit.

'I'll just have a glass of tap water thanks,' said Five.

The waitress flicked her nose up at him and tramped off towards the bar.

Their noisy neighbour was now serenading them with the sound of tearing gristle as he decorated his serviette with crab shell and red wine spittle.

Jax lent further across the table, closer to Five. 'What are you doing over—'

The conversation was interrupted by a tapping at the window. Five looked up to see Tina and Ross staring down at him. *Fuck, fuck, fuck!* Tina mouthed something which he couldn't make out so he just waved and turned back to Jax. *Please don't come in. Please, please.*

Tina did come in. So did Ross.

'What the hell are you doing here mate?'

'Eating… or not.'

'Who's your new friend?'

'This is Jax, we're on a date.'

'What's the food like here?'

'It's supposed to be awesome,' said Jax. 'Why don't you guys join us?' –turning to Five – 'if that's cool with you?'

'Sure, but I really don't think you'd like the food, Tina.' Five looked at Tina with pursed lips and drilled his head from side to side like he was trying to get a bee out of his ear. It was a gesture that Tina knew only too well: it was Five's very subtle way of telling her to fuck right off.

'Rubbish, you know I love seafood. We can have a double date?' said Tina.

Say this isn't happening.

Tina hung up her raincoat and perched herself next to Jax with a big smile stamped across her face. Ross had two seating options: 1) a seat next to Five, or 2) wedge himself against the window next to Tina and forego the ability to breathe. He chose the second option.

'What you two up to?' asked Five.

'We're going to pop into the Electric Ballroom, I want to get some props ready for the tournament,' said Ross not even looking at Five, instead draping his arms around Tina, like a fox fur scarf but twice as sly.

You two are together then.

'So, have you managed to get a residential visa to live over here?' asked Jax.

Noooo don't ask me that.

'Er... Yeah.' Five picked up the menu yet again. 'The wild boar's supposed to be good.'

'What?' said Tina seemingly unable to assimilate that information.

Ross put his happy face on.

'I was looking into it myself, it's not as easy as you'd think for US citizens.'

'I'm good with applications,' muttered Five from behind the menu.

'You are certainly good at making things up,' said Ross.

'What, like health problems you mean?'

Ross's face did an impression of the Titanic and sunk.

'I suppose being the number one tribute band helps too?' said Jax.

Five looked over at the fish tank, pretending not to hear.

'The only problem with that though,' said Ross, 'is that you're not – I am.'

'We'll see about that, won't we?'

'Hey what does it matter?' said Jax, raising her voice. 'We're all just Numan fans aren't we?'

'Yeah,' Five and Ross answered in unison.

'Some more than others,' finished Five, before turning his attention to Tina. 'How's the course going?'

'Great,' Ross winked at Five. 'I've been helping her with her homework.'

'I can speak for myself.' Tina disentangled Ross's arms from around her neck. 'I just started my dissertation, it's a bit of a challenge, to be honest.'

The grazing hog – oblivious to anyone around him – produced a guttural, self-satisfied belch. Five could feel the moist warm air on the back of his neck. His shoulders almost touched his ears.

'So when can I come and see your studio?' asked Jax.

'Priceless,' said Ross throwing his head backwards. 'Is that the one in your mum and dad's conservatory?'

You bastard.

'You don't know everything about me.'

'You're a proper *Mystery*, aren't you?'

Don't you fucking dare!

'I wanna invite to some of your wild parties,' said Jax.

'He might let you change his dad's catheter if you're really lucky.'

'What's up with you guys? Jax's expression nosedived. 'There's a real fucked up vibe between you.'

'Ignore them darling,' said Tina. 'They're a pair of bairns.'

'They're what?'

'All this rutting is about sexual potency and mating rites; they can't even see it. All the talk of the modern man is bull-shit, they're all just little wolves fighting to be the leader of the pack.'

Here we go.

The onslaught was interrupted by the waitress returning

with Jax's beer and Five's tap water. 'Here you go guys.' She turned to Tina and Ross, 'Are you ready to order?'

'The sea bass and a coke, please,' replied Tina.

'The lobster and beer for me, I'm starving.' Ross snatched a toothpick from the waitress's tray and started to dig around in his mouth.

'Looks like we're sharing that little fella over there.' Tina pointed over towards the tank.

Five caught the eye of the lobster again. It was rubbing its whiskers against the side of the tank in counter-clockwise motions. Some sort of code maybe? He felt a tingling at the base of his brain. Could the creature be attempting to tele-pathically communicate with him? 'How do you think that lobster feels?'

'It doesn't,' said Jax, instantly on the defensive.

'That where you're wrong, there are lots of studies that show they feel pain.'

'Really?' Jax tilted her head.

'We treat them like an inert object. Boil them alive and then rip its flesh apart, thinking we're so very sophisticated.'

'It's a fucking lobster,' said Ross, 'who cares?'

'You might one day... when they rise up.'

'Lobsters?'

'No... bigger animals.'

'Elephants?'

'Maybe...'

'Like *Planet of the Apes*?' said Jax.

'With elephants?'

Piss-taking bastard. 'I wasn't being literal. I just mean humans aren't as clever as they think and might get their comeuppance one day.'

'You talk as if you don't belong to the human race,' said Jax.

Five paused to reflect on the question before answering, 'I'm really not sure I do.'

The exhilarating repartee arrived at a lull. Ross started whispering something into Tina's ear and Jax disappeared into her phone. Five got up and strode off in search of the loo. On his way past the fish tank, he found himself face-to-face with the lobster. The desperation in its eyes was amplified through the thick glass walls of the tank. Before he could even think about how to respond, he had reached into the tank, pulled the creature out and smuggled it into the little boys' room.

And so this is where he found himself. It was 8.12pm on a Saturday night. He was sat on a toilet holding a lobster, in a god-awful restaurant, on a god-awful date, sat opposite the woman he loved who was holding the hand of a man he despised. How had life got so out of control? He reached into his combats and pulled out two lengths of bandages to wrap around his new friend's pincers. Making a run for it was his only option. He took off his sweatshirt, wrapped it over the beast and, taking a route via the other side of the restaurant, made it to the coat stand unnoticed. He sneaked out of the front door but before he could celebrate his escape to victory he found Tina waiting for him in the street. She knew him better than he knew himself.

'Hello you.'

'Why?'

'You know why.'

'Why him?'

'He's not as bad as you think he is.' Tina produced a pained smile. 'Not quite.'

'Do you love me?'

'Aye, but I cannae watch you torture yourself anymore.'

'So 40 years and that's it?'

Tina shrugged. 'What about your date?'

'Can you tell her I don't feel well.'

'Why is your sweatshirt moving?'

'I wasn't happy with Jax and Ross's menu choice.'

'This is your chance for a relationship with a beautiful woman and you're going home with a lobster?'

'She could see straight through me.'

'You don't know that.'

Five flipped his collar up and lent over to try and kiss Tina. She stepped backwards and shook her head. They stood staring into each other's eyes for a few moments before Tina shivered and pointed that she was going back inside.

There was one last chance to say something before she disappeared.

'Can you take lobsters on the tube?'

13

REAL LIFE

6th December

'What if everything you knew about reality was wrong? What if you found out you were being digitally manipulated by a superior race of beings that live in a parallel universe? – which quantum physics has proved by the way. What would you do?'

Beep – a pack of kiwi fruit-flavoured Durex passed over the scanner.

'Dunno,' replied the lady on the checkout. Beep – a bumper carton of orange juice. 'I'd probably get out of this shit-hole.'

It was 8am. The sky was as stained and torn as creepy Jenny's curtains. A fierce wind had picked up every stray piece of litter and sent it spiralling down the high street like confetti. Pete was coming down from an all-night chemically induced love voyage to the outer limits of human consciousness. What better place to be than in the refined splendour of a Dagenham pound shop?

Beep.

A tin of hair spray.

'The thing is' – Pete tapped manically on the counter – 'we've all got to find a way out of these government-forged mind manacles... subvert their dominant paradigms... only then will we see the truth.' He lent across the checkout, his eyes spinning vortices of cosmic energy. 'We are interconnected dream weavers spinning an infinite web of love, know what I mean?'

'Yeah, problem is, my Harry's pension doesn't kick in for another five years. I've always wanted to go on a cruise, but he gets seasick so we're buggered either way.'

'Ever-shifting sands... the bastards think they've got us trapped.' Pete stuck two fingers up at the security camera, then lowered his voice, 'Don't worry sister, I have it on good authority the reptilians will be arriving soon.'

'The little boy next door has got one of them bearded dragons, he's right proud of it. His mum hates it though, stinks the place out, it does.'

Beep.

Five packets of Pro Plus.

Beep.

A bottle of budget cider.

Beep.

Two-for-one pack of eye shadow.

Beep.

A dog collar.

Beep.

A black and red tutu.

'Getting ready for a fancy dress party?'

'Every day darling' – Pete stuffed the haul into his rucksack – 'every day.'

∾

There had been movement in the dark underbelly of the virtual reality that holds humanity in its spell. Pete had beckoned Five to meet him in Dagenham Park on their favourite bench. They used to bunk off school and smoke weed on the very same bench. A new café had opened nearby which would enable Pete to piggyback on their Wi-Fi. If you need to hide, do it in plain sight.

The ropes flapped wildly against the park's maypole, but no one would be dancing today. Not far from where they sat, on the largest expanse of green, a local residents' committee had organised a fundraising event for the parish church. Superior beings would have postponed it for a fairer day but the committee had decided it should carry on regardless. Smiling into the eye of a hurricane, as English tradition dictated. It was at least agreed that the skittles competition would have to be abandoned but packing up the bouncy castle would have signalled defeat. Rather like if Churchill had negotiated with Hitler. The vicar had come up with the initiative of allowing twice the safe capacity of kids onto the hovering structure to prevent it from taking off.

'Do we really have to keep meeting outside?' Five tightened his scarf round his neck, sat down next to Pete and rammed his hands between his legs.

'We've got to keep 'em guessing brother,' said Pete. 'We're onto something big.'

'You've found out about their gigs?'

Pete shook his head and smiled, 'Something *much* better.' He reached down into his rucksack and pulled out the bottle of cider as well as two stained mugs. 'Fancy a tipple?'

'Go on then.'

Glug, glug, glug. Jittery arm jerks always plagued Pete's comedowns, making it tricky to pour accurately. Half the cider lined the bench slats, fizzling into the bitter swirling wind. Five swigged down as much as he could manage. Battery acid would have tasted better, but it would help numb the cold. Five's attention was captured by the hysterical children falling over each other on the bouncy castle. It then switched to their parents who drank takeaway lattes and discussed school holiday survival tactics.

'Do you ever feel like real life only happens to other people?'

'There's nothing real about that life,' said Pete, looking over at the crowd and frowning. He flapped open his laptop to allow the screen's glow to light up his bloodshot eyeballs. He placed his most treasured book on the bench next to him –*The Slavery of Our Times* by Leo Tolstoy –and used it as a mouse mat. He used it to create a figure of eight with the cursor as he gathered his thoughts. 'From now on I'm gonna send all my texts from an anonymous server; do you have another phone you can use?'

'Don's got an old pay-as-you-go?'

'You know I said this went deep brother?'

'Yeah...?'

'I was wrong.'

'Huh?' Five pulled up closer to Pete and put his glasses on.

'It goes deeper.'

'How deep?'

'I'm thinking… Illuminati.'

Fuck me he's getting worse.

Five flicked his eyes skyward. 'Look I just want to find out how many gigs they've done.'

'That's the weird thing, the bot's been coming up blank on the band all week, then as soon as I put his actual name in I got this.' A document popped up – it had three letters at the top: A.T.F. and beneath it two boxes for a username and password. 'It intercepted an email en route to Ross via the undertaker's website. It was from a blank source… an email address that expires as soon as it's sent something.'

'Can you open it?'

Pete rubbed the back of his neck, 'I've not seen anything like this before, it's multi-encrypted, it must contain some *heavy* shit.'

'Huh?'

'Standard crack-ware is useless, but' – Pete's face sparkled with possibility as he typed some digits into a code editor – 'I could try… some clone phishing.'

'I'm out of my depth mate.'

'All I need to do is send the same document back to him from another blank source email address but with a tracer to swipe his details when he logs in.'

The cold had sunk deep into Five's spine and he was starting to seize up. He sank the last dregs of cider and squeezed Pete's leg. 'Let's just forget it… we're gonna blow them off stage anyway.'

'Aren't you even a little bit intrigued?'

'Yeah, 'course but—'

'You just asked me about normal life yeah?' Pete wrapped his arm around him. 'Maybe this is what separates us from the herd… we stand on the edge of things looking in—'

'Yeah I know—'

'We don't accept anything blindly—'

'You're always talking me into things I don't wanna do.'

'You don't want to know the truth about this guy?'

'You've always got a fucking answer haven't you?'

'This is how we show our defiance!' Pete typed some more on his keyboard, a pop-up box appeared that had two options: *Enter* or *Return to Safety*. 'This is how we make a difference. It's now or never brother.'

Five reached over and held his shivering hand over the mouse, just above Pete's.

The cursor hovered over the enter button.

The hysterical children tumbled and yelled on the bouncy castle.

Their parents drank lattes and discussed school holiday survival tactics.

Together they pressed *Enter*.

FIVE'S DIARY

10th December

5.30 am

Couldn't sleep at all last night. The cranes were making those bizarre noises again. I looked out the window and they were flashing lights, one after the other, like they were communicating with each other. It weirded me out. I was half expecting the police to turn up this morning. How could I be so gullible? Pete can play me like a fiddle. He's been doing it since we we're 15. I should have got savvy to him years ago. What is he getting us wrapped up in?

7 am

I've just checked my Instagram profile, Ross has left a comment under a photo of me singing. It was done through Tina's account but it's got to be him, he said I look more like Mr Bean than Gary Numan. What a tosser. How low is it to stoop to petty tactics like that? That's what teenagers do isn't it? I'm 56 for fucks sake. I'm not going to rise to it.

7.20 am

I did rise to it. I said it's better than looking like a paper mache Ken Dodd.

8.30 am

Got another postcard today, same as the last one except this was written in it, 'Once a secret sees the light of day, the pain fades faster than a horse drawn sleigh' Pete swears blind he didn't send the last one so it must be Tina. It's exactly the sort of arrogant thing she does. A few months at college and she reckons she can cure the world. If anyone needs to look in the mirror and check their integrity, it's her. And if I didn't know better, I'd think she was trying to sabotage my date the other night. She needn't bother, I'm perfectly good at doing that myself.

9.45 am

Can't stop thinking about Tina and that wanker together. It's getting a bit compulsive. It reminds me of this guy I met after a gig once, he must have been about 50, he was a biologist and went on these expeditions through remote rain forests. He discovered a new species of wasp in Peru which was named after him. How cool is that? I bumped into him in town the following week and he was bent double, walking like an old man. He told me he had got a letter from his ex-wife and that was how it affected him. I couldn't get my head round it at the time. Now I can. When you love someone that much it seeps into your bones. It's hard to ever truly get them out of your system. What gets me is why did she have to pick that sneering tosser? A man so utterly fascinated with the glory of his own existence. I wish he lived in a rain forest.

8 pm

I caved in and read one of mum's articles from the hairdressers. It was about redefining male identity. It was trying
to put forward an argument that masculinity is naturally
morphing into being more emotionally expressive and
creative. It was saying that men feel much more able to cry
these days. I found it all very encouraging, though I'm not
sure their definition included social anxiety and self-pity but
it's definitely a step in the right direction.

12th December

7 am

I had a really weird lucid dream last night. I was alone in a
deserted street, it felt like Romford but I couldn't recognise
anything. There was a figure up ahead in the mist and I'm
sure It was the old lady that's been following me. I tried to
run in the opposite direction but the ground was filled with
these little neon wires, writhing in all directions. One started
crawling up the back of my leg, its little wire pincers digging
into my flesh. Before I knew it, they were all over me, trying
to burrow their way into my ears and mouth. I screamed and
woke myself up. It freaked the living shit out of me. I told
Don about it and he said our unconscious often plays out fear
patterns in dreams. That makes sense but it doesn't explain
the one I had last week about Robert Smith chasing me on a
space hopper.

6.15 pm
    Stubsy just called round, he had a spare ticket to go and
see Uriah Heap and wanted me to go. I respectfully declined.
I've tried to educate him in the past. I lent him my *Metal
Rhythm* CD. I thought because it had the word metal in it he

might go for it. He just told me he does listen to it but only when he's entertaining the ladies in his van. He reckons it helps with his rhythm. I can't believe we have a roadie who uses the Numan's music, something that should be treated as sacred, as a bonking click track. He's a bloody animal. We need a new roadie.

8 pm

I seem to spend my days wishing things were different. I wonder if you ever reach a point where you don't want something else? I've been getting flashbacks again (I just wish I could get past it) Mum keeps asking when my next counselling appointment is. The tournament is next week, everything will be fine after that. I listened to *Pornography* by the Cure today, I still love that album. It simultaneously fills me with despair and hope. Ross said on Twitter he only ever listens to Numan so I replied with an adapted Kipling quote. 'What do they know of Numan who only Numan know?' I was pleased with that but got nothing back. He's a total philistine.

9 pm

Truth is I'm shitting myself about the gig. I would never tell the others that but there's so many variables playing live and this time the stakes have never been higher. I hope we get a decent sound engineer and Don doesn't break any guitar strings! There is NO WAY dad is wearing that fucking slipper on stage. If scientists found that thing at the bottom of the ocean, (good hiding place?), they'd probably classify it as a new species. I keep hiding it and mum keeps finding it, (tracking device maybe?) It's probably just the hum it gives off. I'm sure it winked at me the other day.

9.30

I think Dad has sussed that the burgers I'm giving him aren't meat. It was only a matter of time. Also, I might be paranoid, but I could swear I smelt bacon in the kitchen when I got back from shopping this afternoon. Maybe Stubber's been smuggling it in? I need to get those security cameras installed.

14

WHEN IN ROMFORD

13th December

'I can't get in the bath because there's a lobster in it!'

'Yep, I think I'm going to call him Colin.'

'I bloody stink.'

'We'll have to strip-wash you won't we?'

'What time's the newspaper guy coming?'

'Soon, let's get a shift on.'

'Is it even safe to go in the bathroom?' Frank grabbed the *TV Times* from his bedside cabinet and rolled it up.

Five shrugged. 'You'll find out won't you?'

Candice had called in a favour with a mate of hers that worked at *The Romford Gazette*. She'd managed to wangle a feature on all the bands taking part in the competition. Five had been up most of the night writing down what he wanted to say – he'd written close to ten thousand words. The more profound his sleep deprivation had got the more abstract his ideas had become, until it had turned into more of a philosophical treaty on the art of Numanoidism. As far as he was concerned, though, it was the little details that could make all the difference. Especially in the event of a tiebreak. Imagine that. The Romford Bombers versus The Storm Troopers. Five versus Ross. Numan versus Numan. In two days there would only be one Numan standing (apart from the actual Gary Numan of course). Time constraints had seen today's interview organized as a working breakfast and Don had kindly offered to make vegan pancakes for everyone.

By the time Five had got his dad downstairs, the journalist Mr Pinner had arrived and was sat at the kitchen table chatting to Mags about the horrific thrip damage his roses had suffered last season. The kitchen smelt of burnt toast and grumpiness. Stubber looked dapper, though. He had on his skin-tight Black Sabbath T-shirt, perfectly moulded to fit his pecs. His Levis had been through the washing machine and he'd even trimmed his goatee. This was a clear charm offensive. Don leant against the fridge, fully immersed in the nowness of mixing batter. Five had told him it was vital to whisk for exactly two minutes. Don didn't need a timer though – for, as we all know – time is an illusion. The batter would reveal itself as ready when the conditions allowed. Mags was sat at the table, organising her wool into similar-sized bundles. She'd had to double her efforts to get her present for Five ready in time for the tournament. It was going to be a bright yellow tank top. She was hoping he'd wear it onstage. Five was bound to be delighted.

'Morning everyone,' said Mr Pinner picking up his suitcase and clonking it on the table. 'I thought we could stay in here if that's OK? It will be a nice homely feel for the photos.'

Frank's wheelchair made a crackling noise as it ran over the warped edges of the lino. Five parked him next to Stubber.

Mr Pinner had the misfortune of a deeply engraved grimace etched into his face, making it hard to tell if he'd just had some very bad news or was constipated. He flipped open his suitcase and had a good rustle around whilst muttering to himself, 'Hmmmm… no… I… think we're all tickety boo.' He reappeared, holding a brand-new notepad and proceeded to scribble at the top of it, trying to get his pen to work. 'I bet you're all getting excited now?'

'We were sorting out my keyboards yesterday,' said Mags, 'they're making me sound like a flange.'

'A flanger, it's an effects pedal Mum.' Five winked at Don. 'Rehearsals are sounding good thanks.'

'You're a family band, is that right?'

'I'm Frank Watts, this is my wife Mags and my two sons, Don and Five.'

Stubber reached his calloused hand across the table for a handshake that almost brought tears to Mr Pinner's eyes. 'I've been their roadie for the ten years, ever since the first battle of the bands.'

'There seems to be quite an active Gary Numan fan club round here. Is there a camaraderie with the other bands playing in the tournament?'

'You could say there was' – Mags stared at the stony faces sat round the table – 'a… friendly rivalry.'

'We filmed The Storm Troopers rehearsing for the website this morning. They're a great bunch of chaps, aren't they?'

It was Mr Pinner's turn to stare at the stony faces.

Don scooped up some batter with his ladle and slowly poured it into the frying pan. It sizzled as it hit the hot iron, filling the air with a steamy vanilla aroma. He rescued a spatula from the heavily-stacked drying rack and reached in to the pan to flip it. Hey presto. The perfect pancake. Made with divine love and served with a heavenly aura. Just so it can be devoured and defecated out again. What a timeless teaching on the truth of impermanence! Don placed the first one on a plate for Mr Pinner and poured lashings of honey-flavoured sweetener' on top of it. 'Blessings on your meal.'

'Oh lovely.' Mr Pinner exchanged his pen for a knife and fork and began to wolf down the treat in front of him.

This gave Five the chance to check his notebook; he'd forgotten most of what he'd written last night already.

'How come we're not being filmed?' asked Stubber.

'We only had space for one band and I think our editor took a shine to the singer Ross's blue hair.' Mr Pinner held back a belch and then mopped up the juices dribbling down his chin.

'I know for a fact he made himself go bald on purpose.' Five pursed his lips, nodding meaningfully to himself.

'Why would he do that?'

'So he could have a transplant and be more like Numan.'

'That's quite an accusation,' said Mr Pinner picking up his pen and holding it at the ready.

'It's true though,' said Mags. 'He had 'is barnet done by Shirley, my hairdresser, about a week before 'is transplant and she told me he had a full head of hair.'

Finally, someone is on my side. Thanks Mum.

'How do you make yourself go bald?' asked Frank with a mouthful of pancake.

'I did some research as it happens,' said Five referring to his notebook again. 'Soya sauce has got phytoestrogen in it which kills hair cells. If you rubbed enough into your head you'd be Yul Brynner in no time.'

'If that's true,' said Mr Pinner, 'it says a lot about his commitment.'

'Or 'is desperation?'

'This is *friendly* rivalry, is it?' Mr Pinner scribbled into his notepad in much the same way that Mr Morris used to scribble in his detention book – with a certain arrogant pride. Five took a deep breath and tried to focus himself – there was a lot at stake and so much he needed to get across.

'You have been going the longest of all the bands,' said Mr

Pinner.' How do you see your current status going into this year's tournament?'

'This is a seminal event. As true Numanoids, we showcase the early electro hits alongside his recent industrial rock output, and so make no mistake, we are the most successful Numan tribute act and we are in the driving seat—'

'Although you lost to The Storm Troopers?'

'Listen... last year was a blip, our record speaks for itself. There's only two bands in this tournament—'

'I've got down six here—'

'With a chance of winning—'

'The judges might not see it that way—'

'Let me tell you something. On 21 July 1978 my neighbour Jenny brought round Tubeway Army's single *Bombers* and it blew me away so much, the very next day I put an advert in the paper for guitarists to form a tribute band. Numan then went electronic of course so I had to get rid of them and get keyboard players in, but my point is, I've been here since the beginning. Ross rocks up a year ago and struts around the place like he's King Numanoid.'

Mr Pinner held his pen vertically in front of him and waved it as if he had an important point to raise. 'Speaking of electronics... this last question is a bit awkward but I have to ask you about a rumour going around that you are in a relationship with one of these new AI robotic love companions?'

Five's chin dipped. 'How did you find out about that?'

'We were emailed a somewhat revealing photograph.'

'You need to keep that out of your fucking paper, 'said Stubber. 'There'll be a media shit storm!'

'You need to be a celebrity for that…'

Cheeky bastard.

'Aren't you supposed to be helping to promote us?'

'That's what I'm getting at. If anything, this would help with publicity.'

'What are they talking about love?' Mags' eyebrows drew closer together.

'She was an electronic love doll.' Five avoided his mum's gaze and stared down into his lap.

'So, you admit it then?'

How can I deny it?

'It was an accident.' The sinews around Five's jaw tightened.

'You didn't know you were having sex with a robot?'

'She was made of silicone... I was very drunk.'

'That's pretty rock n roll,' the journalist smirked to himself as he jotted away in his notepad.

'I've read they've got whole brothels of sex robots in America,' said Frank, 'they're all at it over there.'

'If you're looking for an angle to sell your fucking paper you can forget it,' Stubber's eyes protruded from under his wiry eyebrows. He rarely understood the situations that Five got himself into, but it never stopped him being protective.

'It was that sad bastard Ross that sent you the picture wasn't it?'

'We can't reveal our sources I'm afraid, although I have to say you do seem a bit obsessed with him.'

Bollocks.

'What makes you say that?'

'You can't stop talking about him.'

'I'm just telling you what he's really like.'

'But it's not fair is it? He's not here to defend himself.'

'I don't ever want that sad twat in my house.'

'Some people might say being in a rock and roll band with your parents is a bit sad.'

Stubber cracked his knuckles and kicked the leg of Mr Pinner's chair. 'Are you taking the piss?'

Don tried to defuse the situation by plopping a pancake onto Stubber's plate.

'I'm... merely stating a fact.' Mr Pinner's hand started to

wobble. 'I won't be intimidated from discussing difficult issues, this is my job.'

'Have you ever heard of a man called Jess Lidyard?' Five crossed his arms.

'No.'

'He was Gary Numan's uncle and he was also in Tubeway Army, so now tell me how sad it is to have your family in the band?'

'That's quite different to having your mum and dad in the band though isn't it?'

Don, having served up all his pancakes, thought it a good time to address the room. He put his hands in prayer position. 'Can I remind everyone that what we all ultimately want in life is what's best for ourselves *and* each other. I know we all get caught up in our worldly pursuits but they don't last. The only things that endure are the seeds of our karma that go on to rebuild our next incarnation.'

Everybody nodded in silent agreement, even though they looked a little unsure about what it was they were nodding about.

'I'm sorry Don,' said Stubber, 'you are right. I wish I could be more like you. Would you teach me how to meditate?'

Don beamed like a microwave oven. 'Of course. Speaking of which, you'll all have to excuse me, it's time for my morning meditation.'

As soon as Don had levitated out the room, Stubber picked up his pancake and hurled it across the table straight into the journalist's face. 'What do you think of that you muppet?'

Mr Pinner sat frozen to the spot, unblinking as bits of mushy pancake slipped down his cheeks into his facial crevasses. He jumped up, slammed his suitcase shut and ran for the front door. Stubber decided it only proper to chase after him, waving a saucepan dripping with pancake batter. After a moment's reflection, Five thought he should probably try and stop Stubber, as pulverizing a journalist to death – however justified – might be frowned upon by the judges, not to mention the police. Morality is such a messy business.

By the time Five had calmed Stubber down and got back to the house, Mags and Frank were in the conservatory, lost in musical oblivion. They were churning out a rendition of Ricky Martin's 'Livin' La Vida Loca' with Frank on vocals. Britain's definitely got talent. Mags shouted over the music to Five, 'What do you reckon on this for a cover version? Get 'em dancing at the end?'

Five closed the door and walked down the hallway to his bedroom rubbing at the crease of his arm. He grabbed his rucksack containing his paragliding kit and threw it over his shoulder; he needed to clear his head. He would get up as high as he could into those clouds and soar like an eagle again. First, he had to feed Colin and hide his dad's slipper.

BRIAN'S BOOTS

Brian

Hi, I saw your Ad. I've got a spare set of boots, I'm not sure they are exactly what you're looking for but you are welcome to them.
08:41

Five

Cool! what are they like? 08:46

Brian

Thigh-length PVC 5-inch platforms with studded straps all the way up. They are bondage boots really. I had them hidden in the airing cupboard but my wife found them and she's got the right hump. I've got to get rid of them pronto. 10:48

Five

Perfect! when can I collect? 10:49

DEAR GARY

I hope you got my last letter. It's the battle of the tribute bands tomorrow night, we had our last rehearsal today and we've never sounded better (even if I do say so myself). I think you'd be proud of us though. There's so much riding on it for us. I don't know what I'd do if we lost. I'm quietly confident we won't though. It feels like my destiny. It will be so great to meet you properly. There's so much we'll have to talk about. I know you don't fly anymore but I go paragliding sometimes. I'm sure there's other stuff too. I know you are rehearsing for your tour at the moment but they're filming the competition so I hope you get to see us play. I'd also love to know what you make of The Storm Troopers. I think they're a pile of wank.

Five.

P.S. I don't know if you get invited to a lot of parties in L.A. but if you ever go to one and someone offers you a tampon love bomb, please just say no!

133

15

HOW THE WORLD WORKS

14th December

Camden Town is a crawling beast.
A crouched figure in a derelict doorway.
A peephole.
A steaming turd.
A damp bedsit.
A guestlist.
A soaring bliss.
A hungry ghost.

R ound the back of The Electric Ballroom was a small, unlit alley where shifting shapes morphed in the darkness. Their footsteps crunched over broken glass as they looked for the delivery entrance. Exhaling a frosty breath, the Count switched on the light from his phone to reveal a narrow red iron door. The lock had rusted, and the key was hard to turn. Ross had to lean hard against the frame until it clicked. They picked up a handle each of the holdall and dragged it into the venue. The air was thick with stale body sweat and the residue of crass chat up lines. Ross switched on the lights and pointed over to the steps leading up to the balcony. As they heaved the bag upwards, the muted clank of metal against concrete echoed over the dance floor.

'Are we the only ones here?'

'Should be, it's closed tonight.'

'How did you get the keys in the end?'

'Her mother in law snuffed it last week, and I gave 'em a deal to get 'em onside.'

'That was handy.'

'I told her we needed to get our *stage props* up.'

'Huh huh.'

Once on the balcony, Ross unzipped the bag and took out some metal poles. Squinted at an instruction leaflet, he carefully pieced them together.

The Count grappled with a bulky object in the holdall – the veins in his temples bulging – he yanked at it, tutting to himself. It was another five minutes of colourful language until the head of the exquisite Mystery popped out. 'I turned the sound off, she's proper fruity isn't she?'

'She's gonna be a superstar tomorrow night.' Ross let out a short gravelly laugh.

'If we'd been given the green light none of this would have been necessary,' said The Count, removing his leather gloves.

'Don't get me started on that, sooner or later you have to start taking matters into your own hands.'

'Where we gonna hide everything?'

'There's some lockups underneath the lighting rig, apparently. Where did you put the sail cloth?'

The count grabbed Mystery by the feet and dragged her toward the other side of the balcony. Her long blonde hair fanned outward as her head bobbled up and down on the beaten up floorboards. About halfway round, the balcony light came on and a middle-aged man in overalls appeared, holding a mop and bucket.

'Alright mate?'

The Count stared at him.

'I'm the cleaner.'

'Ah, right.'

'You playing tomorrow, then?'

The Count nodded, trying to edge past the man without pushing him over.

'I'll be there.' The cleaner put his bucket down and used his mop to lean on. 'I'm a massive Numan fan as it happens.' He took a crumpled rollie out from behind his ear and stuck it in the corner of his mouth. 'I've seen him live 132 times.' He pointed at the Count and chuckled, 'Now tell me I'm not a fan. He's cost me a bloody fortune actually.'

'That's great but—'

'The first gig I ever went to was in 1977, it was in Crackers nightclub in Soho, do you know it? If memory serves, the band he was in was called… Riot. I remember he turned up in a brown Ford Granada, he was wearing black jeans and—'

'Listen I'm—'

'I actually worked with Gary at Woolworths for a while too—'

'That's interesting but—'

'Did you know he's got webbed feet? That's where his family name comes from. I've got a picture on my phone if you want—'

'I really don't have—'

'See, what a lot of people don't realise about Numan is that he's not like other humans, in some ways he's—'

'Right, well it's been great talking.' The Count pushed past the man and carried on his way.

'Hang on' – the guy pointed down at Mystery – 'what's with the sex doll?'

'Well… er… its…'

There was a loud thud and the cleaner bent forward grabbing at the back of his head. Behind stood Ross, holding a metal pole.

'Aww, what the fuck was that for?'

'You won't knock him out with that,' said the Count.

'Why not?' said Ross.

'Hang-glider poles are hollow, aren't they?'

'Why do want to knock me out?'

'What choice have we got?' said Ross lifting up the pole again.

'I won't tell any—'

Whack.

'SHITTING FUCK that hurt!'

'Maybe if you hold two poles together,' said The Count, 'and hit him hard on the temple?'

'That could kill me!'

'Alright, on the back of the head, but hurry up we've got to get this rigged up.'

Whack, whack, whack.

'FUCK ME.' A small stream of blood ran down the back of the cleaner's neck.

'Did you bring the wrench?' asked Ross

The Count nodded and wondered off to look for it.

'You can't use a fucking wrench.' The guy shook his head in disbelief. 'Are you *trying* to kill me?'

'Have you got anything in your cleaning cupboard we could use?'

'I think there's a mallet in there but look, if I don't mop the dance floor tonight, I'm gonna lose my job.'

'Are you seriously trying to strike a deal with me?'

'You help me, I'll help you. That's how the world works

isn't it?' The cleaner took out his hankie and held it to the back of his head.

'Is it?' said Ross, like it was an alien concept. He sighed heavily, 'how long will it take?'

'Half an hour tops... less if you give me a hand.'

'Are you taking the piss?'

'How about you sweep and I mop?'

'I don't believe this.' Ross stared at the guy with his mouth open. 'Right OK, but I'm gonna knock you out *as soon* as it's finished.'

'That's fine.' The guy picked up his bucket and gestured to Ross to follow him as he set off towards the cleaning cupboard. 'So where will you put me when I'm out?'

'Dunno. Probably in a coffin in the back of our hearse.'

'Will I be able to breathe in there?'

'For fuck's sake, all you do is try and knock someone out and you get the bloody third degree!'

The guy stopped under the lighting rig and pulled open the lid of a large metal container. 'Why don't you put me in one of these? They have built-in ventilation and I could even stick a few seat cushions in the bottom'.

The Count arrived back and passed the wrench to Ross. Without a moment's thought and with an almighty crack he struck the guy round the back of the head and pushed him into the container. 'That's how the world really works mate.' He pulled the hankie off the back of the guy's head and used it to wipe the blood stains off the wrench. 'And tomorrow night Five is gonna learn the same lesson. I can't fucking wait.'

16

NUMAN VERSUS NUMAN

15th December

The Bombers hit town at 5pm, just in time for the soundcheck. Stubber's transit van rattled to a weary full stop outside the venue and Five wound down the window to inhale the biggest lungful of London he could muster. A whole lifetime waiting to be defined by a single event. No pressure then. Camden High Street was bursting with Numanoids, an army of the dispossessed who had come to bear witness - to pay homage – to the one who would claim the most hallowed crown of electronic mimicry. Every square inch of wall space was lined with posters upon posters advertising the next musical spectacle coming to town. Five took out his phone and snapped a picture of the venue's neon sign, 'The Electric Ballroom'. It shone down on him like an interrogation lamp. This was it, boys and girls. Time to fulfil your destiny.

Stubber had been well schooled in the art of lugging amps and setting up equipment and it was for this reason the band couldn't survive without him. It bought the rest of them valuable time to find the dressing room, source inadvisably salty snacks and, most important of all, take some Dutch courage. The image Five had in his mind of their dressing room was the kind you see stage actors being interviewed in. Brightly lit dressing tables strewn with makeup, rolled up ten pound notes and copies of posters to sign for adoring fans. Where they found themselves, in reality, looked suspiciously like a storage room. Though, to be fair, someone had gone to the trouble of placing five warped plastic chairs in front of the stack of aluminium beer kegs.

'Maybe there was a mix up?' said Five, trying to get comfy but failing. 'We passed a lovely dressing room down the hall.'

'This'll do, love.' Mags plumped up the cushions she'd brought along and lined her chair with them. "least it's got a loo.'

'I'll order us some drinks,' said Frank, wheeling himself off down the corridor. Don followed closely behind him; he wanted to find a quiet nook to practice some pranayama. After all, if you go on stage with your chakras out of kilter how can you possibly expect a higher rebirth?

Mags and Five were unpacking their stage gear when Candice strutted in. 'Evening all.' The glare from the bare light bulb glimmered on her bared tusks as she hooked out a chunk of crisp with a newly lacquered fingernail. Spotting Five, she walked over to him and dropped her head to a forty-five degree angle.

'Alright babe?'

'Yeah.' Five looked up and smiled.

'Sure?' She placed her salty fingers on his shoulder.

He nodded, furrowing his brow.

'Everyone's been chatting shit about you on Facebook ain't they?'

'Huh?'

'They've been calling you a sex pest' – Candice tilted her head even further to make clear her concern – 'you poor love.'

Five dug his nails into the layers of hardened chewing gum stuck to the bottom of his chair.

'Let's hope you give a good account of yourself tonight yeah? Prove 'em all wrong.'

Mags tapped him on the shoulder and mouthed, 'Ignore 'em, bunch of wankers.'

Frank returned, this time with Stubber in tow, holding a large tray of drinks.

'Now we're talking.' Mags gave her husband a big smacker on the forehead. 'I need a little livener, my back's bleedin' killing me.'

Frank grinned and reached down into his knackered duffle bag, pulling out the smartest item of clothing he possessed. It was a traditional Spanish Yucatán shirt he'd bought from a tour he did in '78. It hardly screamed industrial rock but it was better than his old Stevie Nicks T-shirt that smelt of cabbage. The shirt had two top buttons missing, which revealed a king-sized portion of grey man-chest. Every band needs at least one sex icon.

Five sheepishly unpacked the giant lump of a bondage boot and hauled it across the room to drop in front of his dad.

'What the bleedin' hell is that?'

'It's your stage gear.'

Frank picked it up and stared at it like it was an alien being.

'All the alternatives are wearing them.'

'I'll look like a bloody golf bag, are you gonna be my caddie?'

'You can't wear the slipper' – Five shook his head as if was of the gravest of concerns – 'not tonight dad.'

'While we're on the subject…' Mags proudly presented her son with the bright yellow tank top that she'd been slaving over for the last month.

Five had hoped she'd forgotten to bring it. *Fuck me sideways.* 'Thanks mum it's lovely.'

He held it up against himself and tried to figure out where the arm holes were.

'It gets proper toasty under those lights mate,' Candice chimed in, 'you'll get too hot in that.'

Genius! Five looked over at Candice and thanked her with his eyes. She had a heart, after all.

'I'll have to be careful then,' said Frank, winking at Candice. 'I've had excessive body heat ever since snorting cocaine off a groupie's thigh backstage at a Fleetwood Mac gig.'

'You mean "Brentwood Mac" the tribute band,' said Mags, 'and it was my thigh.'

''Don't ruin it for me,' said Frank whilst tugging at the straps and zips on his new boot.

Candice plonked herself down next to Five, and like a passport control officer flicked through the sheets on her clipboard. 'The judges have asked me to go through a bit of admin with you. There's two new rule changes this year. The first is that all the singing must be live. You'll remember from last year we had to disqualify the Iranian act "Garytollah Numeini" for lip syncing.'

'We don't do 'nuffin like that,' said Stubber ripping the lid off a can of lager.

'I know babe, but I still gotta tell ya. The second is that ninety per cent of your act must have been written by Gary Numan himself. So, if you wanted to do a song he co-wrote we would have to work that out as a pro-rata percentage. Everyone gets three songs and you lot are on second-to-last as you came runners up last year. The Storm Troopers are headlining—'

'For the last time,' said Stubber.

'We've sold out tonight, fifteen hundred people, it's our biggest crowd yet.'

Five looked over at Mags and puffed his cheeks out – he had always dreamed of doing a gig this big. He never really believed it would happen.

'Lastly, we've got a new Welsh acapella act called The Barry Numans, they do the singles. I just heard them sound-check, *amazing* voices.' She raised her hand as a witness. 'It was proper spiritual, know what I mean?'

'Oh I'd like to see them,' said Mags.

'You better hurry up then, we're putting them on first before anyone turns up.'

The light from the hallway was obscured as a dark figure entered the room. It was none other than Pete, bedecked in full-body rubber suit and a studded dog collar. It was a special occasion after all.

'Captain cosmic has arrived, everyone,' said Stubber, announcing Pete's arrival with a curled upper lip.

'You're wasted as a security guard,' said Pete as he fluttered past him.

'Watch it, you.'

Pete jumped on Five's lap with a thud and wrapped his arms around him. 'Big night, brother!' He pulled a photocopy out of his man bag and handed it to him, accompanied by his finest Cheshire cat grin.

Five's face lit up. 'Everyone remembers we're starting with Pete's poem don't they?'

'I read it,' said Frank, 'it's *really* deep man.'

Responding to a crackle on her walkie talkie Candice headed over to the door where two aged rotund men lay in wait. 'In you come boys.' She banged her clipboard on the back of a chair. 'This is Mr West and Mr Morris, tonight's judges, they've come to introduce themselves.'

With no seats available, the judges hovered in the doorway awaiting a lull in the myriad of conversations. Seizing the initiative, Frank swept his hair back and wheeled himself over for an introduction. 'Hello I'm Frank Watts, the drummer.'

'Good to meet you – Nigel West.' The judge offered his hand to Frank. 'We're all looking forward to tonight.'

Frank gave him a wink. 'Any relation?'

The judge narrowed his gaze. 'To whom?'

'Fred?'

'No.' Mr West retracted his hand.

Frank wheeled himself back across the room.

After a quick round of introductions, Mr West came – not for the first time – face to face with Pete. This prompted a theatrical display of consulting his wristwatch, tutting and then making a sharp exit. That left Mr Morris to address his captive audience. Being a Mussolini of the natural sciences, it was an activity he was well accustomed to. He stood before them in all his glory – a mass of sweat and cholesterol attached to a rigid waxed moustache. Old shit pits. He looked like an offcut of ham in a corduroy suit, precariously held together by a single lard-splattered button.

'I'll be the second of your judges this evening.' He linked his fingers and rested his arms on the apex of his stomach. 'I don't normally listen to popular music but rest assured I judge on categories ranging from technical ability through to melodic composition.'

'That gives us an edge,' Five whispered to Pete.

'Do I know you boy?' Mr Morris turned to Five, peering down over his metal-rimmed spectacles. 'You look very familiar.'

Five shook his head and stared even deeper into the floor than usual. 'I think I just have that kind of face.'

'Well, I best be off, it's time to introduce the first act, best of luck all,' and with that Mr Morris waddled off down the hall towards the stage.

'Do you think he recognised you?' asked Stubber.

'Not sure.'

'What was that smell? asked Frank.

A deafening roar from the crowd cascaded down the hallway as Mr Morris began his opening speech.

'Good evening everybody and welcome to the tenth – and final – Battle of the Gary Numan Tribute Bands!' He paused for the crowd to erupt again. 'Tonight, the ultimate tribute act will be chosen!'

A surge of electricity shot up Five's spine; he pushed Pete from his lap and sprang to his feet.

'I'm shitting myself, but I can't wait to get on stage.'

'Do you need to borrow my catheter?' asked Frank, causing the room to explode into laughter. A precious moment of light relief, shattered instantly when two people entered the room. Tina and Ross.

'Hi lovelies, it's great to see you all.'

She was wearing that faded *Pleasure Principle* T-shirt that Five had bought her on their tenth anniversary. She'd cut the sleeves off to make it look more unique. Ross stood close behind her stroking the tops of her arms. A sight that sent shudders through Five.

'Bit pokey in here, innit?' said Ross. 'You should see our dressing room – velvet seats, the works.'

'We're alright thanks,' replied Frank.

'Evening Ironside, good luck tonight, I hope you don't get a puncture.' Ross released one of his self-righteous sniggers. He looked so pleased with himself as he looped his arms around Tina's waist. Tina immediately stepped forward to unhook herself.

'Too easy mate,' said Frank putting down his can of lager. 'Let me give you a little music history lesson. Ever heard of Rick Allen?'

'Nope.'

'Def Leppard's drummer, one arm.'

'And?'

'Waylon Jennings, a country legend, one foot missing.'

145

'Fascinating—'

'I'm not done yet... Jerry Garcia, guitarist in the The Grateful Dead, two thirds of his middle finger missing in action and I'm not even going to mention Stevie Wonder.' Frank wiped the phlegm from his beard as Stubber placed himself strategically in front of his wheelchair. Coiled and ready to pounce.

'Is that your guard dog?' Ross nodded towards Stubber.

'What did he fucking call me?' The dark purple veins in Stubber's neck began to swell.

'I didn't hear 'im properly,' said Frank, growing braver in the safety of Stubber's shadow, 'it sounded *a bit* like he called you a cunt.'

Stubber looked ostentatiously over his shoulder at Frank, 'He called me a fucking cunt?'

Frank nodded slowly with the gravest of expressions.

'*No one* calls me a fucking cunt!'

Sensing the imminent risk to her new boyfriend's life, Tina pulled Ross backwards to the door. 'We only came in to wish you all luck.'

'Piss off!' Stubber marched towards them, sending them scurrying down the hall like whippets.

'I can't bear to see them together,' said Five, looking at his mum.

'I know, love.' She put her hands on his. 'You channel all those feelings into the show tonight and let's make this the best show ever.'

Stubber was about to the slam the door when Bhagwan Don appeared, chakras realigned, glowing like the Brighton Pier on a summer's night. 'We're on in ten minutes everyone.'

Shit! The dressing room erupted like a disturbed ant's nest, everyone running into everyone else. Five saturated his head with nuclear grade hairspray: one last attempt to force his hair into submission. Mags was squeezing herself into leopard-skin leggings. The Tina Turner look was exactly what could swing it for tonight's crowd.

Stubber swaggered into the centre of the scrum, dragging the steel caps of his cowboy boots across the floorboards for effect. 'For ten years I've been driving you lot about, hauling heavy amps, getting home at 3am on a work night, having my wife accuse me, unjustly, of running around with groupies.'

Everyone tried desperately not to look at anyone else.

He stamped down hard on the beer-stained floorboards. 'And do you wanna know why?'

There was a mass shaking of heads.

'Coz' I fackin' believe in you!' His eyes were welling up, in spite of himself. 'There's also something I haven't told you' – he bit into his clenched fist – 'Rambo has got worse, he's really sick at the vets… I'm not sure he's going to pull through.'

'I'm sorry Stubsy.'

'So can I ask you all a favour?'

Everyone nodded like novelty toy dogs.

'Will you go out there, play like I know you can and win this tournament for Rambo?'

'Yeah!' everyone howled in unison.

Leading The Bombers down the hallway to the stage, Five noticed a lump obscuring the stage door: Mr Morris. He tried to scurry past him unnoticed but a hand grabbed the top of his arm. 'I've just worked out who you are, boy, Bobby Watts!' He peered down at Five – close enough to see the beads of sweat bubbling out like popcorn from the ridges in his leathery forehead. 'I often wondered what happened to you. I've been hearing some very disturbing rumours about you, boy, I knew you'd never come to much but you seem to have sunk to new depths.' He took out a monogrammed handkerchief and splattered the contents of his nose into it before pushing Five aside and trundling out onto the stage.

'Please welcome your next act, Five Watts and the Romford Bombers.'

Five turned to his bandmates, flinging his arms up in despair.

'Ignore it,' said Don rubbing his back, 'we're gonna win this.'

Five composed himself and stepped out into the bright lights; it was like entering heaven. An ethereal hum from the guitar amps crackled in the background, the smell of spilt beer and the cool rush of dry ice came cascading in from the sides of the stage. Lazer spotlights splintered off the polished steel frame of the drum kit. Don, Mags and Frank took their positions and began readying themselves as Five approached the microphone.

'Good evening everyone,' he cleared his throat to steady his warbling voice. 'We're going to… start with a poem.' Five's hand was shaking so much he pushed it hard against the microphone stand to keep the photocopy steady. Pete had printed the poem in big letters so he didn't have to break the spell of rock mystery by putting reading glasses on.

'Who am I? I am the timeless one that moves between worlds… watch me as I fly above the clouds and shape your reality. Then just when you are not expecting it, I'll fade away. For I am the Urban Alien and this apocalyptic wilderness I call home. My painted face is the war cry of the gods… I can handle anything now.

When the time comes, we're gonna rise up and take down the electricity grids—'

'Where you gonna plug your girlfriend in?' someone shouted from the audience.

Five reached for the crease of his arm.

'Just carry on,' shouted Don.

'Bugger this!' Frank signalled Mags to start the bass line to the opening song, 'My Shadow in Vain', before counting them all in. 'One, two, three' and – bang – the Bombers were in session. Man did they sound good! In fact, they sounded amazing, better than Five could ever remember; fresh, vital and in time. Mags' keyboard through an effects pedal didn't sound half bad either. The audience swelled forward, rising and falling like waves. Moving as if one living creature. Frank resembled animal from the Muppets, all elbows and spinning drumsticks. A furball in his own private rock nirvana. He was stamping away so fiercely on his bass drum he nearly put his big toe through the end of his slipper. There was a dizzying display of keyboard prowess from Mags – She was old school, yes, but schooled she was and this was a lesson in how to set melody free. On the other side of the stage, looming out of the dry ice, the Bhagwan was pure focus, each note perfectly executed, every chord stupifying. For him – this moment – was all there was. These lights and this sound. An immaculate display of Zen and the art of Numanoidism. Five's whole skeleton felt like it was vibrating with ecstasy. This was all he ever wanted, the only medicine he'd really needed. This was pure oxygen for his soul.

The one protection you have against a fickle crowd is to make your music talk. The Bombers were making it scream with ecstacy. The song ended with a frenzied roar from an audience demanding more. Frank raised his drumsticks in the air and counted in Don for the opening guitar riff on 'Are You Real?' At the front of the crowd and wailing at the top of his voice, Stubber was head banging with wanton abandon, 'I fucking love the heavy stuff!'

Nestled next to Don's amp at the side of the stage, Pete was filming the action on his phone whilst simultaneously eyeing up a guy in the audience. Who said men can't multitask?

The new song brought a change of lights. Red laser beams shone down, dissecting the dry ice and causing Five to look up and notice something on the lighting rig above. It looked like someone had climbed onto it and was hoisting up a large object from the balcony. He could only make out blurred outlines as the lights changed again into an intense white fluorescence. He wasn't sure whether he was imagining it – being the surreal occasion it was – but it looked like the object was moving towards him. A few in the crowd stopped dancing and pointed upwards. Inaudible gasps and shouts emitted from their open mouths. It was then the object dropped past the lights into plain view. It was Mystery. She had been gaffer-taped to a small hang-glider and was careering towards the stage like a meteorite. By the time he had realised what was happening it was too late. Mystery hit him full force in the chest, hurling him backwards across the stage where he hit the deck with a numb dull thud.

For a few moments the rest of the band stared in shock. Stubber shook them awake by climbing onstage and grabbing the microphone. 'Who fackin' did that?' The crowd looked back at him, ashen faced.

Five was out cold. Mags stood over him screeching at the audience, 'Is there a doctor in the house?'

'Everyone clear out the way.' Candice appeared from the wings holding two bags. 'I'm a qualified first aider yeah?' She plopped her Gucci handbag down – in full view of the audience – and unzipped a large green first aider's bag. 'Let's get him in the recovery position.'

Stubber ran backstage to find the stairs to the balcony. He was followed by a very out-of-breath Mr Morris who was yelling something about health and safety considerations.

Five came round ten minutes later in the dressing room, surrounded by his entourage. Candice was just about to give him mouth to mouth. A small mercy. He grabbed the back of his head and winced.

'Are you OK love?' said Mags, the tears visible on her cheeks.

'I'm alright... bit dizzy... this isn't going to affect our chances is it?'

'I don't think you're going to win babe.' Candice did her head tilting thing.

'Why?'

'Your mate Stubber just headbutted Mr Morris.'

'Why?'

'Stubber took umbrage at being called a preposterous midget. '

'Is Mr Morris OK?'

'He's still unconscious.'

Candice's walkie talkie buzzed. 'Hello? This Frank on security, I've just found the cleaner upstairs in a lockup. He's not making much sense, I think he's in shock, can you come and check on him please?'

'What kind of fucking nightmare is this turning into?' Candice disappeared off in the direction of the stairs, clutching her first aid bag.

Five reached his arms out to Pete to help him to his feet. The room was a merry-go-round, he clung to him like a limpet.

'You need to rest brother.'

'I just wanna get out of here. Get your stuff together everyone, were going home.'

CRASH LANDING

Tina
I'm so sorry. I promise you I didn't know he was going to do that.
I'm really fucked off with him. 03:04

Five
I'm not surprised in the least. 03:10

Tina
If its any consolation, The Storm Troopers were disqualified too
03:11

Five
Who won? 03:11

Tina
The Barry Numans 03:12

Five
Good on them 03:15

Tina

I miss you 03:20

Five

You're still with him though? 03:25

Tina

He's not who I thought he was 03:26

Five

You've made your bed 03:27

FIVE'S DIARY

16th December

4.30 am

When we were leaving the Ballroom last night, I walked past Tina waiting in the queue for the cloakroom. She looked at me and I saw the worst thing imaginable in her eyes. Something I never wanted to see in anyone's eyes. Pity. I've only got myself to blame I suppose. Chasing some mirage of rock n roll happiness at my age. If I'd really thought about it, I could have predicted something like that would happen. None of it matters now though, as I'm going on a little trip. One way.

I'm going to strip naked and walk.
    I won't stop, just keep going till I end up in the ocean.
    The sea will swallow me.
    But I still won't stop,
    I'll sink to the depths,
    New depths, that even shitpits couldn't predict,
    Unfathomable depths.
    Deeper than anyone before me.

To where the Gargoyles live.

I'll join the whales swimming blind through the murky wilderness, calling out to no one.

I'll give myself back to whatever cosmic trickery created me,

Become part of the inexplicably twisted beauty of nature once again.

I can't imagine anything more peaceful.

And maybe then, I'll finally be free of you.

17

UNFATHOMABLE DEPTHS

16th December

The bells on Mags' alarm clock clanged violently as it edged across her dressing table. She was having a rather odd dream that she was the lynchpin of a Venezuelan cartel that smuggled camel wool across the border. It served her right for watching *Breaking Bad* directly after *Knitty Gritty*. She always knew when she was awake – the pain came back. It was like a razor blade crawling up her spine. She lay staring at the Artex swirls on the ceiling, a gooey-eyed grump. When the pain became unbearable she thumped the button on her automatic bed raiser and yanked back the Crimplene bed covers. Once her puffy pink feet had been securely Velcroed into her decrepit nylon slippers, she grabbed her walking stick and tottered over to the window. For the last 40 years she had opened her curtains and cast a keen eye on the seasonal changes to her front garden: the autumnal browning of the birch leaves in the garden hedge; the drift of scarlet from the winter hellebores; and, come summer, how far Frank's disinhibited mint patch had encroached upon the lawn. Today however, only one thing caught her attention and that was her son Five, lying naked in the garden pond.

'Help! Don, quickly!'

Ten minutes later Five was sat on the sofa, wrapped in his duvet and clinging to a cup of coffee like it was a life support machine. The central heating had been turned up to almost twice the permissible level. Two solemn faces sat either side of him.

'I'm gonna call an ambulance.'

'Mum… no.' Five's voice cracked.

'The doctor then.' Mags picks up her phone.

'He'll get the social worker onto me again.'

'You need help, love.'

Don rubbed his brothers back. 'I'm worried about you too.'

Mags pushed down on her walking stick to lift herself, her legs wobbled as she stood upright. She pointed at her mobile phone on the sideboard. 'You're gonna need to give me a very good reason not to call.'

'I'm just upset… last night was shit.'

'That's not good enough love.'

'What do you want from me?'

'You're going to book another appointment to see Mrs Summerisle, and actually turn up this time.'

Five nodded and pulled the duvet tighter round his neck.

'What's going on down there?' Frank called out from the top of the stairs. 'It's like Dante's *Inferno* up 'ere.'

'I need to get that old goat down for breakfast.'

'He can wait,' said Mags attempting a smile. 'You do know your father and I only joined this band to make you happy?'

'I know… it does… it will do.'

'When? It should just be a bit of fun, love, that's all.'

'Mum's right.' Don flicked his Mala beads quicker than usual.

'I thought we wanted the same thing?'

Don paused to collect his thoughts. 'Say… we had got to support Numan. Do you think you'd feel any different about yourself afterwards?'

Five's chin began to wobble.

'We know it's not been easy for you, love' – Mags grabbed his hand and squeezed it hard – 'that's why you need to talk to someone, or it will never change.'

'I know the band's not going to fix my problems… but I can't give up. I can't even explain why… I just know I can't.'

'What are you looking for, love?'

Five shrugged, then dropped his head forwards. An uncontrollable tiredness had come over him.

'I need to lie down.'

Collapsed on his bed and staring at the drawn curtains, he could feel himself drifting from consciousness when there was a gentle tap at the door. This was followed by a ripped page from a glossy magazine being slipped under door.

'Hello?'

'It's only me love. I forgot to say, I got this article for you from the hairdressers. It's a test to see how you are coping… you know, emotionally.'

'I haven't got the energy mum.'

'It's OK, I've answered it for you.'

'Right… how did I do?'

'It says there's a chance you might be suffering from a low mood.'

'I'll be sure to pass that on to Mrs Summerisle.'

Five could sense his mum hovering on the other side of the door.

'Love...?'

'Yeah?'

'Me and your dad have always loved you... just the same as Don. You know that don't you?'

'I know Mum.'

'And love...?'

'Yeah.'

'Me and your dad want to press charges against that bastard.'

'Don't worry about him. Revenge is a dish best served cold.'

LUNATIC FRINGE

18th December, 7.30 a.m.

The growl from the industrial estate had crept into Five's dreamscapes and dragged him back to Romford. That dip in the pond had left him with a man flu more severe than any known disease. He had tried to get up once already, but the world had turned kaleidoscopic and so he resigned himself to floating in and out of a Lemsip-induced delirium. Just before closing his eyes he noticed he still had a photo of Tina on his dressing table. It had been taken by Jenny next door, just after they got together all those years ago. That was in an entirely other world. A world that never failed to seduce him.

It was 24th May 1979, Gary Numan had just reached number 1 in the charts with 'Are Friends Electric?'. Having just watched this monumental tune being performed on *Top of the Pops*, Five – then known as Bobby – ran upstairs to raid his mum's makeup box and put on eyeliner for the first time. It was a seminal moment, a postmodern rite of passage which gave rise to a profound euphoria (and conjunctivitis). Five the rock star – formally known as Bobby – had never quite grasped the thinking behind his given name. Why, when there had been a profound tapestry of English poets, artists and explorers, had he been named after Bobby Moore the footballer? Even if he had been the captain of *that* 1966 England team. They could have, at most, made it his middle name.

After an enthusiastic application of foundation, lipstick and blusher, Bobby looked at himself in the bathroom mirror. What stared back at him was his distorted twin, a twisted alter ego who would be strong enough to overcome any obstacle in life, clever enough to subvert any restrictive societal code, a persona who would ultimately guide him to the promised land of fame, riches and happiness. Electricity ripped through his body. This kind of rhapsody could only come with having discovered his true purpose. His DNA had been engineered exactly to do this and nothing else. He knew his destiny was to be in the world's leading Numan tribute band and nothing would stand in his way.

It was his seventeenth birthday and Mags had given him twenty quid to treat himself. Pete had come round and they were going to London to an alternative nightclub called Billy's in Soho. They had read about in the *New Musical Express* and it seemed to be where the cutting edge of the post-punk vanguard were hanging out. They took an early train to London to give themselves a chance to soak up some of the city before the club opened at midnight.

'I sense a good night coming on,' said Pete, dumping his dirty DM's on the seat opposite.

'The bright lights... the glamour.' Bobby was crouched forward trying to use his window reflection to do his hair.

Soho was insane, a circus of sex shops, spice bars and strip clubs. It was lit up like a Christmas tree and the air was saturated with fast food aromas – not the usual smell of fish batter

– but exotic spices, a cacophony of brand new smells that set Bobby's senses alive. To many, back then, Soho was the ring-piece of London; to these two it was a romantic wonderland that held an ocean of possibilities on every street corner. Even the reek of piss-drenched back alleys seemed in some way heady, bohemian and invigorating.

'Let's have Russian food… no Turkish… no Japanese!' said Pete.

'Whatever your heart desires,' shouted back Bobby as they darted between the gridlocked traffic on Wardour Street. They were heading for the sanctuary of Otherworld Records, an indie record shop, where they spent three hours searching for any new bands that might have so far alluded them. Pete was mad into an experimental counter-culture band called Throbbing Gristle and worshipped their lead singer Genesis P-Orridge. It didn't take him long to find a kindred spirit in the store's proprietor. A young guy who was wearing a ripped Crass t-shirt and had a long line of connected safety pins dangling from his right ear lobe.

'Did you see the performance art show they did?' said the guy. 'It was wild.'

No, I'm gutted I missed it,' said Pete. 'I've been trying to get hold of the soundtrack.'

'I've got the bootleg out the back, I could do you a copy if you like?'

Pete ran over and threw his arm around Bobby who was busy trying to work out of he could afford to buy the new Bauhaus single and still get shit-faced that evening.

After a late dinner consisting of a shared bowl of MSG-laden stir-fry, it was time to find their way to the nightclub. Entering Dean Street, Bobby passed an open door leading to a stairway within. A sign pinned to the door frame read 'Model Upstairs.'

'Do you reckon there's a prostitute up there?'

'Why don't you go up and see?' said Pete

'I'm not fucking desperate.'

'But you *so* are,' said Pete chuckling to himself.

Tuesday nights at Billy's nightclub was Bowie night and it was the one stop shop for the artist, the dispossessed, the misfit, freak or anyone with any kind of radical agenda. It was a much needed refuge for those who dared to be different, including but not limited to: a six-foot body builder in army boots and a wedding dress; a lady in her sixties wearing flipflops and a bin liner; a bloke with a papier mâché teapot glued to the top of his head. For Bobby and Pete, it was filled with the bizarre and sympatico friends they had not yet had the pleasure of meeting. As they stood in the long queue of subterraneans waiting to get in, the pair discussed philosophical hot potatoes, such as: how do you know if you are having an existential crisis; and how long would the club's transvestite bouncer last in Romford?

Naturally, the club was situated in a basement, beneath what some would refer to as a house of ill repute. It was like walking into Nosferatu's underground lair. Dry ice was being pumped from a rickety old machine in the corner of the room and spider webs made from lace curtains had been stuck to the walls. The smell of nicotine, sweat and cheap hairspray hijacked what little oxygen there was in the club, and the only visibility to be found came from the network of strobe lights hanging from the ceiling. Bobby couldn't believe what he was seeing – semi-naked bodies, clad only in fishnets writhing on the dance floor. The only response the boys could manage was to look at each other and dissolve into frenzied laughter.

It took a mere twenty minutes for Pete to disappear into the toilets with a Bhutanese fireman called Sally. Where's the sense in delaying gratification when it can be found instantly? Bobby checked his makeup on a mirrored wall tile and bought himself a pint of snakebite and black. Scouting around in the dry ice, he managed to locate a seat with a strategic view of the dance floor. 'The Staircase (Mystery)' by Siouxsie and the Banshees was blasting out of the speakers, it's haunting guitar riff sending goose pimples rippling up his arms. He took a long swig on his pint then sat back, trying to look cool, not realising he had just given himself a purple moustache.

That's when he saw her for the first time. She was spiralling in and out of the spiderwebs, her arms splitting the billowing dry ice like a shadow puppet. Alone in the middle of the dance floor, her jet-black back-combed hair was like the crown of an alien goddess. She wore ripped tights and tatty Doc Martin boots with the words 'lunatic fringe' painted on the side in silver. Bobby could feel his pupils dilating; he had never seen a woman like this before, he didn't even know they were physically possible. What struck him most of all, though, was the fact that she looked more depressed than anyone he had ever seen in his entire life. She was utter perfection. Having no way near the prerequisite degree of confidence needed to get within a metre of such a walking miracle, he decided instead to drink himself into an inadvisably blended lager/cider-induced stupor. What if he asked and she said no?

The song reached its blistering finale and she left the dancefloor, heading in the direction of the bar. This was his chance. Following close behind, he managed to jostle a prime position next to her as she tried to get the attention of the barman.

'Who's next?'

Bobby grinned and turned to the mysterious woman. 'You first.'

'Pint of lager please.'

'That'll be 50p.'

'I've only got 40p.'

'Well that's not enough is it?'

'Oh really? I didn't know.' She tutted and shook her head.

Bobby dug into his pocket and handed 10p to the barman, 'There you go.'

'Cheers mate,' she smiled and leaned forward to take a sup from the frothy top of her drink so she could pick it up. It looked like she was going to walk away – he couldn't let that happen. Not after getting this far. And forking out 10p. *Say something!* He noticed she was wearing a purple crystal tied tight around her neck by a leather cord. He pointed to it. 'What's it made of?'

'Are you trying to pick me up?'

Shit, think fast

'No, I'm…'

'I saw you watching me, when I was dancing.'

'Oh.' He felt like he'd been kicked in the stomach.

'Coz if you are, I'm no interested.'

'I'm…'

'Everyone tries to hit on you in this place.'

'I'm not like that.'

'That's what they all say.'

Give me something!

'I'm… looking for members for my new band, we do Tubeway Army covers.'

Perfect!

'Aye, I'm interested in that.'

'Do you play bass?'

'No,' – she shrugged her shoulders – 'but how hard can it be?'

Bobby nodded not even caring what the answer was.

'It's amethyst,' said Tina touching her necklace, 'my dad gave it to me.'

At the end of the evening Bobby walked away with a precious phone number, neatly folded and secured in the zip compartment of his wallet. He felt as tall as Westminster Abbey. The band would be amazing with her in it and he'd get to… well, see her. He went off in search of Pete to tell him the exciting news, but despite looking under every coat and cobweb he was nowhere to be seen. It wasn't until they turned the lights on at the end of the night that Bobby found him fast asleep in a toilet cubical with his trousers round his ankles, clutching what appeared to be a string of Bhutanese prayer beads. Bless him, it had been an awfully long day.

Walking back along Dean Street, Pete stumbling in his wake and the strangeness of dawn above, Bobby felt certain of one thing. This night – and this phone number – were proof that the world could be different and he could be something new. But such a future was not going to happen to anyone called 'Bobby'. As the memory faded, Five reluctantly opened his eyes to greet the dull horror of the here and now. He stared vacantly around his bedroom. His head spun like a washing machine but he had a to-do list twenty miles long. His first task would be the joy of wrestling his dad out of bed. But at least after organising everyone's breakfast and medication he would be free to go and sit in sub-arctic temperatures whilst listening to Pete's latest conspiracy theory. It wasn't all doom and gloom.

RENDEZVOUS

Pete

Still on for tomorrow? 13:55

Five

I've got flu 14:28

Pete

You've got to come, really important news 14:31

Five

have I got a choice? 14:38

aPete

Remember where our 1987 summer school trip was? (Don't write the name) 14:55

Five

No 14:56

Pete

Terry Southurst head butted you and I fingered Kirsty Barton?
14:58

Five

I feel even worse now, how could I forget that !? 14:59

Pete

11am. Make sure not followed. 15:01

19

THE END OF THE LINE

18th December

By the time Five arrived at the Ongar Heritage Vintage Railway Station, Pete was already perched on the platform bench, submerged in his laptop. The glare from its screen lit up his green hair which, fought for attention with the vermillion paintwork of the steam train behind him. It was a miracle Five had made it, given the creeping fog in his lungs and the fact his brain felt like it was slowly ebbing out of his nasal cavities.

'How you feeling?' Pete pulled down his face mask.

Five looked across the station with a thousand-yard stare before replying, 'Like I've had a frontal lobotomy.'

'Least it's not raining!' Pete grinned and closed the lid of his laptop.

Five grunted and sat down.

'I've got some mental news brother.'

'What?' Five rubbed his legs vigorously to try and keep warm.

'Not here' – he put a finger to his lips – 'I've got us tickets for the choo choo.'

'I'll be sick if I go on one of them.'

'Trust me brother, it will be fun!'

Five turned around to look at the steam train behind them. It had been so lovingly renovated and polished that it glistened, even on a day like today. 'They have done it up nice,' he conceded. 'I think it's the same one we went on with the school trip, innit?'

'Yeah... but' – Pete pointed towards a rusty carcass on wheels at the other end of the station – 'we're on that one.'

Fuck me.

'Great.'

'It's perfect brother, no one ever goes on it. We can set up a hot spot from my phone.'

'We're gonna freeze to death, can't we go and sit in the park?'

'Too many eyes, brother.'

'Where?'

'The bushes.'

Five shook his head and wiped his dribbling nose with his sleeve, 'How long is this gonna take?'

'Alright, stroppy.' Pete pointed to the hipflask in Five's combats. 'What you taking?'

'Painkillers and hot toddy, but they're hardly making a dent.'

'Ketamin is supposed to be good for Flu, I've—'

Five picked himself up and strode off towards the train muttering a creative range of expletives to himself. A plaque on the side of the train door read 'SECR Wainwright P-class'. After a couple of concerted tugs, the door creaked open and, as it did, the tops of his boots were decorated with a pile of iron filings, rust and paint chippings. He climbed in and plonked himself on the wooden slatted seat, pulling his legs up in front of him so he could hug them. It was dark, cramped and reeked of coal dust. It reminded him of the time he and Don used to hide in their grandfather's back garden bomb shelter.

'This was built in 1910, incredible hey?' Pete parked himself opposite and began unpacking his digital gadgets, spreading them over the seat beside him 'You're not going to believe what I've got to tell you.'

'Morning lads.' A ruddy-faced conductor with faded tattoos on his hands stepped into their compartment. 'Just you two today is it?

'Hang on,' said Pete flicking through his phone.

The conductor lent forward to ogle at Pete's gadgets. 'You a journalist?'

'I'm writing a novel on the gender diaspora and the death of patriarchy,' replied Pete, winking at Five.

'Right you are mate,' the Conductor quickly stood up straight again.

Pete held up the screen of his phone to show their tickets, puffing out his chest for a performance of the only celebrity impersonation in his repertoire: that of a camp Brian Blessed. 'Good sir, with this bill of sale we command your iron steed to ferry us across this green and pleasant land. And whatever you do, please do not stop until we reach the end of the line.'

The conductor, stony faced, turned to Five. 'How do you put up with him?'

'If you are referring to *me* my good man,' replied Pete, still in character, 'my pronouns are they, their or theirs.'

'How many of you are there?' said the conductor, who had seemingly spotted an opportunity to try and be funny. 'Do you need more tickets?'

Pete raised his eyebrows, looking at Five and reverting to type. 'This is patriarchy in action brother.'

Five took a swig of hot toddy and turned to stare out the window trying not to smile. It was his intention to remain in a foul mood all day but Pete, damn his eyes, always found a way to cheer him up.

After a sustained period of what Five regarded as very unnecessary whistle blasts, the train reluctantly pulled away from the station.

Ca chunkca chunka , Ca chunkca chunka.

The seats trembled with the grind of steel-on-steel. Steam slinked past the window like a phantom snake, before dissolving into the bitter air.

Five hugged his knees as tightly as possible. 'Couldn't you have picked a train with heating?'

'I've only got past the first layer of encryption,' said Pete looking up from his screen, 'but, the bastard fell for it.'

'Huh?' Five threw his glasses on and snatched hold of Pete's laptop. It was the same 'A.T.F.' document he'd already seen but now it had a line of text below it which read:

For the attention of Agent Patterson. Enclosed is the revised schedule of operations re. the Alien Task Force.

'What the fuck does this mean?'

Pete's eyes revolved in their sockets. 'It's what I've been *telling* you brother!'

'"Aliens" as in illegal immigrants?'

'Wah-wah!' replied Pete as phlegm rained from his mouth. 'This is all about shape-shifting reptilians, how many years have I been telling you about them?'

Five took another long swig on his hip flask. 'I don't think I've been listening.'

'This is proof!'

'That he's an immigration officer?'

'That he's a government agent.'

Five handed the laptop back to Pete. 'I think we've been

had, this is exactly the sort of prank he would pull just to show us up, isn't it?'

The light in the carriage dimmed as the train entered the thick canopy of Epping Forest.

Ca chunkca chunka, Ca chunkca chunka.

Sparks from crushed gravel danced outside the window like fireflies.

'Can you get into the rest of the document?'

Pete pressed his lips together. 'Nope, but I do know of someone...'

'Who?'

'I don't know how safe it is to—'

'Who is it?'

'He's a bit of a mythic figure on the dark web, he's a master hacker.'

'If he can help, get him on board. As far as I'm concerned, I wanna take Ross down and I don't care how many gigs they've done or what we're even looking for anymore. I just wanna take him down.'

'He goes by the name of Ghost Hunter.'

As soon as the name had left Pete's lips, the computer screen went dead and the train's brake let out an ear-splitting screech. The carriage juddered violently, sending the contents of Pete's rucksack skittering over the carriage floor. Five and Pete grabbed hold of the overhead luggage racks as the screeches grew louder and louder until a final jolt – and then silence.

'You OK?' asked Five as he knelt down to help Pete scoop up his belongings.

Pete looked Five hard in the face. 'We need to get out of here NOW, brother.'

They crept out of the carriage and into the next, making their way to the driver's cab at the front of the train. Pete cranked open the door – the heat hit them square in the face. The door to the firebox was open. Lying face down on the floor was the conductor with his arms splayed out beside him. Pete knelt down and grabbed his wrist.

'I think he's still alive.'

'I'm calling the police.' Five dug through his pockets for his phone. Before he could find it, there was the loud crash of a door slamming in the adjoining carriage. Footsteps could be heard running towards them.

'Fuck!' Pete dragged Five toward the door and together they leapt down onto the train track.

With no time to discuss options, they disappeared into the dark embrace of Epping Forest. Running blindly through the pine trees, branches jabbed at their torsos, brambles tore at their legs. Behind them, the voices of men shouting, followed by the echoing crack of gun shots. Bullets split the air above them. Five was on empty, it was only Pete's alarming silence that kept him running. They ran and they ran, all the while knowing all it would take was one lucky shot and this would truly be the end of the line.

20

THE FINAL NAIL

18th December

It was 6.30 on a Tuesday morning and Lance Bamford had just yanked his four-year-old son Tyler out of bed and stuck him in front of a bowl of Coco Pops. He then sprinted round the house with a to-do list that would make War and Peace look like a Post-it note. Running up the stairs, he stubbed his big toe on the stairgate, which catapulted him into a Cro-Magnon warrior dance on the landing. As he spun in circles holding his foot, he cursed his brother for booking such an early slot at Tanera Mor funeral park. Today they were burying Lance and Trevor's mum – known locally as Granny Bamford – God rest her soul. She was famous in Romford, having worked in the fish market for fifty-two years. People used to come from as far as Barking for a tub of her jellied eels. Candice had gone ahead to the park to check they had got the flower display right for the wake. They were expecting at least five hundred well-wishers, so everything had to be military precision and Candice was just the woman for the job. It took her all of a minute to have the manager pinned up against the wall with a clipboard flapping in his face.

'When they bring in the coffin, I want the spotlights, slide show and the organist to start playing at the same time yeah? 9 o'clock sharp yeah? I want it proper spectacular.' She stretched a lump of spent bubble gum out of her mouth and lowered her voice whilst staring the manager hard in the eyes. 'You see... my Lance has problems showing his emotions and he's been lower than a worm's tit lately.' She bit her lip and fanned her eyelids. 'I think... the more dramatic it is the more... therapeutic it will be for him, know what I mean babe?'

'Of... course madam.' The manager swallowed what looked like a cue ball and adjusted his cuff links.

'Also, I'm getting my nails done at eleven firty.'

Five miles down the road Stubber slammed the front door to his council flat, tightened up the hairband on his greasy pony tail, pushed out his pecs and stared up at an opaque sun looking for gaps in the clouds. This was a brief respite in a punishing schedule. His responsibilities included: part-time security guard; part-time roadie; bodybuilder; procurer of borrowed goods; carer for a diabetic chihuahua and a full-time fucking legend.

He knew almost nothing about Gary Numan's music, but had seen Status Quo sixty-three times, so stick that in your vaporiser. It's not easy finding the time for philanthropy, but Stubber always showed willing, like the time he donated two quid by text to an army veterans' charity. Or when – out of solidarity with his wife – he gave up porn for lent. Gandhi would have marvelled at such altruism.

Today he'd found a window to follow up on his promise

to Five to acquire a new synthesizer for The Bombers. As he swaggered down the road towards the town centre, his stonewashed jeans flapped in the feral wind. He stared down to admire his neatly ironed turn-ups which – due to a combination of ageing and heavy weightlifting – seemed to grow a little higher with each passing year. He reached the corner shop on the edge of the high street just in time for a beam of light to break through the clouds and illuminate the pollution-smeared grime covering its windows. Huddled in the shop doorway, and wrapped in a threadbare sleeping bag, sat a middle-aged man with a faraway expression. He was holding a cardboard sign that read, 'I bet you ignore me.'

''Ow much?'

'What?' The guy wiped his face.

'How much do you bet I ignore you?'

'Everything I've got.'

'What's that?'

The guy rifled through the change in a woollen cap in front of him. '£1.36'

'So how are you feeling today?'

'Alright… bit cold.'

Stubber scooped up the cash and carried on his way.

After another twenty minutes of assaulting the pavement with his cowboy boots he came to an abrupt halt. He had a quick glance up and down the high street, then ducked down the side alley behind Wright-Patterson Funeral Directors. It was obviously rubbish collection day as he could hardly move for dustbins and recycling boxes. The fetid odour of composting food hit him first, followed by an acrid undercurrent of stale milk. He stood, holding his nose and staring up at the rear wall of the undertakers. There was a gate but it was blocked off by stacked packing crates; the only way in was over. The wall must have been at least six foot high. Not an easy climb, especially for someone who was, perhaps, not quite as tall as other people. He slipped on a balaclava, dragged a couple of bins together and used them to hoist himself onto the top of the wall. The coast looked clear, so he launched himself over and landed in the middle of a flower bed. He found himself in a little courtyard amongst bits of coffin lids and all sorts of keyboard circuitry strewn about. The undertaker's itself was an old redbrick Victorian building that had started out as a school, then became a workhouse and now served the dead, as if consciously following the passage of human life. Being an aficionado of the craft of lock-smithery, it took him the grand total of three minutes before he was inside the vestibule rustling through drawers and emptying coat pockets. In front of him was a large oak door held up by wrought strap hinges. He carefully turned the ring handle and slowly pushed it open. It creaked loudly and he paused, trying to adjust his eyes to make out the contents of this dimly-lit room.

After a few moments, he stepped inside, causing dust particles to collide like asteroids in the thin shard of light from the rear window. Finding the light switch, he realised he'd hit the jackpot. *Yes.* A whole rack of synthesizers lined the wall. Rather than grabbing one and running, however, he found his attention taken by a packing crate in the centre of the room. It was overflowing with masses of small spindly wires; like shiny slow-worms, nearly transparent save for a murky substance inside them. Stubber reached into the crate and, amongst the wires, found a piece of broken panelling. It looked like a type of alloy but it was as light as a feather and covered in thousands of tiny indentations – some kind of synth circuit board maybe? He then wandered over to the work bench on the other side of the room. Next to a heap of electrical parts lay a small aluminium casing; it had a row of antennas attached to one end and the initials I.S.B printed across its surface. It reminded him of when he used to take his transistor radio apart when he was a boy. He had just taken out his phone to snap some photographs when he heard voices travelling quickly down the corridor toward him. Without thinking he grabbed the smallest synthesizer he could find and hopped into a coffin that was laid out on a bier close to the door. He found himself cheek to cheek with the cold, moist, wrinkly skin of a corpse. But it was too late – the voices had entered the room.

'Who's left the lid off the fucking crate again?'

'Don't look at me.'

There was a slam of wood against wood. 'We need to get a lock on this.'

'Now?'

'Nah, Granny Bamford needs to be up there for 9am, her daughter-in-law is a right ball-ache, she was giving me her life story on the blower yesterday.'

'Do they think we're counsellors or something?'

There wasn't much room to move in the coffin – the sides had been stuffed with the wires and panelling from the packing crate. Stubber could feel a vibration as the men fiddled with the lid. His face slipped down the side of the corpse's oily cheek, exposing an intoxicating reek of rotting flesh. So dense a bouquet you could have cut shapes in it with a knife. He tried not to breathe but couldn't stop himself gagging, 'huuuk.'

'What was that?'

'Just the corpse… they make all kinds of noises. One of them farted the other day while I was trying to eat a cheese sandwich.'

'Bloody disgusting.'

Then there was a clicking noise which sounded like the metal clasps being fastened either end of the coffin.

Shit they've locked me in!

The footsteps of a third person entered the room, which was followed by a muffled exchange in what Stubber thought might have been Spanish. Though, being the cultural aficionado that he was, it could just as easily have been

Japanese. The footsteps retreated and there was a bang on the coffin lid.

'On three, one, two and up.'

'Fuck me! she weighs a ton.'

'We had to really stack this one… we're not shifting enough apparently.'

'Another directive?'

'You know we're getting another delivery in today?'

'Someone should tell them there's only so many dead people. This is gonna put my back out again.'

Stubber could feel the coffin being lifted, a giddy sensation, a knock against the door frame and a drop in temperature as they left the building – then a thud as he was slammed into the back of some kind of vehicle. The wires lit up with the impact, creating a mini florescent wonderland. 'Shit!' A shiver ran through him as he noticed Granny Bamford's eyes were open. *Aren't they supposed to close them?* Stubber couldn't reach far enough to peel the baggy skin down over her bulbous eyeballs, so he would just have to put up with her gawping at him. The coffin shook with the vibration of the engine starting. He couldn't think straight, he took out his vaporiser and started chugging furiously, to try and mask the smell as much as anything. *I wonder how much oxygen I've got left?* He hooked his phone out of the top pocket of his denim jacket. It only had 3% battery left. Catching Granny Bamford's eye, he nodded his head in acknowledgement, 'Yeah yeah, I know I should have charged it.' He brought up Five's number on speed dial. It might last long enough for one quick call. Maybe.

Brring, bring.

Pick up.

Brring, brring.

Fucking pick up.

'Alright Stubsy?'

'I'm in a coffin.'

'You a goth now then?'

'This is serious. I'm locked in a coffin, in the back of a hearse about to be buried or even worse... fucking cremated.'

'Wha—'

'Will you take care of Rambo if I die?'

'What are you talking about?'

'If I don't text you by midday, find out where Granny Bamford's buried and come dig me up.'

'Where's Granny Bamford now, then?'

'I'm on top of her.'

'That's a new low—'

'Not like that... my battery's about to—' the screen went black.

'Fuck, fuck, fuck.'

Maybe this was it. Stubber dropped his head in resignation, resting his brow on Granny Bamford's oily chin. Of all the scrapes he'd been in. All the ways he could have died. He was going to get buried alive. Perhaps it was karma, whatever that was. He remembered Don trying to explain it to him once but he thought it wouldn't affect him as he'd never been to India. Either way the game was up and, to make matters worse, he now felt a fresh urge to throw up. The coffin rumbled and jerked, shook and shuddered as the hearse roared down the motorway. Stubber was turning a colour not dissimilar to that of his coffin sidekick. There was a churning in the pit of his stomach and bile crawling up his oesophagus. A spasm ricocheted through his abdomen but before he could decorate the inside of the coffin, the vibration calmed and the vehicle began to slow. Eventually coming to a halt. The rear door creaked and there was the sound of approaching footsteps, crunching across gravel.

'Morning Mr Bamford, we're really very sorry for your loss.'

'Thank you, Mr Patterson.'

'There's a few details we'd like to go over with you quickly if that's OK?

'Can we take Mum into the reception room first?'

The coffin rose again, more footsteps and opening of doors. A warmth, the gentle clack of wood on wood and the slow fade of voices until, silence. Staring deep into the sunken eyeballs of his coffin companion, Stubber gasped, 'you're right grandma, perhaps this is my last chance to get out, it's been a fucking blast though.' He then felt motion around him, the wires had started to move. They wriggled and slimed over Granny Bamford's withered body, revealing thin metal pincers with which they tunnelled into her eyes and ears. *Fuck me!* He quickly twisted himself around until he was facing upwards and started kicking. Short jabs at the bottom of the casket lid with this steel-capped boots. Crack, crack, crack. And with biceps engaged, he pushed upwards with all his might. *If I can bench 300 pounds, I can bloody well do this.* He heaved and spat, and to celestial sounds of cracking bones beneath him, eventually felt the lid move as the clasps started to give way. One final shove and bingo! The lid went soaring through the air and crash landed at Candice's feet who was sat in quiet contemplation with all of Granny Bamford's grieving friends and relatives. Candice jumped up and screamed, 'Lance! Lance!' as the outline of Stubber's dumpy figure rose up from the coffin, covered in glowing red wires, through a blueberry & cheesecake vape mist.

The vicar collapsed in a heap in front of the floral display and the organist sprinted off in the direction of the fire exit, while the rest of the audience looked like they had been collectively hypnotised. In one last flurry of exertion, Stubber launched himself from the coffin and landed with a hollow thump on the wooden staging. It was at that moment the Bamford boys came running into the room looking a little less than pleased with the situation.

'Fackin' get 'im!' screamed Lance.

Stubber picked up the synth and bolted out of the exit as fast as his compact legs would ferry him. Lance and Trevor ran after him like a pair of rabid sabre-toothed tigers with extreme antisocial tendencies. Candice checked her clipboard, then her watch, and tutted. If the boys weren't back soon they would miss the start of the slide show. The nail salon was chock-a-block until the new year and there was no way she was waiting that long. She cleared her throat and turned to address the audience. 'Can someone *please* wake the vicar up!'

DON'T LOOK BEHIND YOU

Pete

I think they might be onto me 10:05

Five

Thought you were untraceable? 10:07

Pete

So did I! 10:11

Five

What do we do? 10:12

Pete

Act like nothings out of the ordinary. Don't tell anyone anything.
Promise me 10:13

Five

I'm scared 10:15

FIVE'S DIARY

19th December

<u>3 am</u>

I keep playing the events of the railway over and over in my mind. I hope the conductor was OK. I made an anonymous call to the ambulance service when I got home. Pete didn't want me to contact the police, he thought it would make things worse. I can't imagine what the conductor's family are going through this close to Christmas. I don't know what Pete and I are getting into, but we're out of our depth. I wanna see Ross fall but was he really responsible for what happened on the train? I so wish Pete would zip it about aliens. That document is probably a hoax, isn't it? What if it's not though? I just did some searching online and you can get undercover immigration officers, it's a proper thing. Could that be what he is?

<u>5.15 am</u>

On the way back from the railway, I saw the old lady again, up closer this time just on the other side of the high street. She must be at least in her eighties, she was staring right at me. I tried to cross the road towards her but the traffic wouldn't let up, she'd gone by the time I got over there. I think Tina was right about one thing. I am living inside an episode of the Twilight Zone.

9.15 am

And yet another postcard! Today's one says: 'Once we truly accept our brokenness, we can broadcast to it the entire universe and no one can use it against us.' I have to admit, I quite like the sound of this one. I'm going to Aldi later, maybe I'll do some broadcasting there? I normally bump into at least one of Mum's friends from the hairdressers. The conversation would probably go a bit like this:

'Hello Five dear, how are you?'

'Fucking awful thanks, I've been awake since 3am consumed with self-loathing, how about you?'

'Er..'

'Have you seen the two-for-one offer on basmati rice they're running this week?'

Whoever is sending these, I can see what they are doing, and it makes perfect rational sense written down. But it completely paves over how debilitating fear is. Fear is insidious, it gets its hooks deep into you and monitors you like a guard dog. That's why I can't jump around screaming my truth at everyone. Anyway, tell me someone who doesn't have secrets.

2.30 pm

Terry from the vegan society just popped in. He's such a top bloke. He's off to visit his mum's this weekend in Margate and so he's going to release Colin the lobster back to the wild.

I feel so good about saving his life. Also Dad is really starting to hum so it's a good job we're getting the bath back again.

4 pm

Mum's spending a lot of time in Dad's room which is giving me a bit of space. I've been having some great chats with Don. We've been chatting about reinventing the band, Mum and Dad will be too old to carry on soon. I think Mum's rubbing off on him too, he always looks so concerned about me. He has a very subtle way of suggesting things through the use of questions whilst acting like he doesn't know where he is steering me. He thinks I don't know what he's doing. I know looking for happiness in fame is a mugs game, I get that. It's just that all my happiest moments in life have either been creating, performing or listening to music. I'm following my joy. Isn't that what we're encouraged to do? The problem is, without the band getting some recognition, how will we ever get to do this for a living? I don't want to be a carer on benefits for the rest of my life.

21st December

3.15 am

I got woken up from the noise from the industrial estate… it's a kind of weird buzzing sound. It's 3am What the fuck are they doing? I just went upstairs for a wee. The landing hallway was an echo chamber of self-satisfied snores, gloriously uniting in one common aim: to piss me off! I don't mean it. I'm glad they all sleep well. Sleep is a like an emotional reset button. It's no wonder I'm all over the place.

4 am

I just listened to 'I, Assassin'. I haven't heard it in ages. It's definitely in my top five Numan albums. Music is my reset button.

5.20 am

I read back over some of my recent diary entries. I get so caught up in my emotional dramas. But they are not the full picture of who I am by a long shot. Underneath I am resilient and have a deep determination pushing me forward. I know I'm meant to do something meaningful in this life and I know it has something to do with music. That's why I can never give up on the band.

8 am

Stubsy popped in on his way to work. He keeps confiding in me about the women he's seeing. His poor wife. If she wasn't already a minister it would be enough to turn her to religion. I hate covering for him. I'm not going to do it anymore.

22nd December

8 pm

I've got a banging headache. I've just had Stubsy ranting down the phone for the last hour. He was apoplectic. Someone has used a stencil to write 'Stubber 100% sucks cock' in huge letters on the wall of the shopping centre loos. All the staff are sharing it on social media apparently. He was asking me what it meant? I would have thought it was fairly self-explanatory. He wanted to know why they'd used a percentage, he couldn't get his head around it (excuse the pun). I suppose they've got a point though, if you just wrote 'Stubber sucks cock', it wouldn't have nearly as much validity. Credit to them, they have obviously given it a bit of thought. Qualifying the phrase with a percentage does make it sound like it has some kind of proof. Like there's some concrete evidence behind it. I didn't even know you could get stencils that big. Anyway, Stubsy is on a man hunt and there's 100% chance he'll find them. That's one stencil I wouldn't like to get caught with. He's also stressed about Rambo who's not making much of a recovery, poor thing. He said something cryptic at the end of the conversation too (my brain was mush by this point) It was about correcting the injustice of the Battle of the Bands. I haven't got a clue what he was on about.

23rd December

<u>3 am</u>

It's Christmas tomorrow. I'm not a big fan. which is not really something you can tell people in polite conversation, that's why I keep it a secret (one of many) I just find it a bit of an inconvenience. All that pretending to be happy. Why should I be forced to celebrate consumerism? The very thing that is driving us all to extinction. If we could be honest for a second about what it actually is that would be something. It is a shameful display of western greed and opulence designed to give the illusion that our spiritually bereft capitalistic culture has substance and purpose, (I'm starting to sound like Pete). What really gets me though is that it's cynically dressed up in pseudo religious fancy dress. Homage to Jesus. A man who would have undoubtedly despised Christmas. Religion is a fairy-tale. Just a story to help people cope with the fear of death. Which is fine I suppose, we all have our coping strategies. (Like I can throw stones at anyone?) But the reality is we're on a spinning rock, lost in space and no one has any clue who we are or why we are here. That's not to say I think it's the end when we die, it's just that I don't think anyone on

193

the planet knows what happens. Apart from Don maybe. Mum says we should feel lucky to have each other, that should be enough. I agree and I'm so grateful for my family. Imagine being alone at Christmas. I wonder how the day affects Jenny? Mum invites her to join us but she always refuses. I'm glad she takes her some dinner over, she's too scared to leave the house apparently. Though saying that Dad has seen her in the park and Don saw her in the corner shop. I guess that makes her a high functioning agoraphobic. Back in the day, she turned vegan before me, she used to spit on the butcher shop window in the high street and not even flinch when the butcher came out holding a bloody cleaver knife. She wasn't scared of anyone. Why do things change so radically beyond our control? None of us really know if we are going to wake up in the morning. That's one of the benefits of insomnia I suppose. I miss Jenny.

21

MINCE PIE PARLEY

25th December

It was another night without so much as the vaguest hint of a delta wave. Five had lay awake regurgitating the events of the last few weeks whilst half expecting the SAS to come crashing through the window. Despite this, he was determined to make Christmas a bearable day for everyone else. The alarm clock squealed at 6am; it sounded as though Mags and Don were already up and clattering about in the kitchen like a pair of disorderly toddlers. That just left Dad to get up. The tingly sweet aroma of mince pies followed him as he clawed his way up the stairs. *Where the hell was he going to get enough energy to last the day?* He flung open his dad's bedroom door to find him dangling out of bed, fiddling with some kind of device. It was hard to make it out as his frizzy mop of hair was hanging down over it. Five knelt down to get a closer look.

'You old goat!'

'How many times have I told you to knock?' Frank sat up looking flustered.

'That's why it's so hot in here.' Five scooped up the device to find it was a small electric heater; he read the label, '2000 Watts.'

Frank smoothed down the left pocket on his pyjama top and murmured to himself whilst trying to come up with a mitigating excuse. He couldn't, so he smoothed down his right pocket instead.

'Hormone problems?'

Frank blinked his big brown eyes, 'I did take cocaine though, ask your mum.'

'Is she in on this too?'

Frank nodded solemnly, scouring his pyjamas for more pockets.

'It's a bloody conspiracy.' Five planted his hands firmly on his hips and shook his head in the sternest of fashions – just like Mr Morris in geography when one of his pupils got confused between a stalactite and stalagmite. 'Do you know how much electricity these things use?'

'We'd all bloody freeze if you got your way.'

'So we'll just starve instead then?'

'Hopefully not today.' Stubber appeared in the doorway with a smile like a hippo's arse-crack. "Appy Christmas lads.'

'Merry Christmas mate!' A wave of relief swept over Frank's face and he raised his arms, signalling Stubber to help him out of bed.

'So, yesterday then?' asked Five looking at Stubber and raising his eyebrows.

'Yeah... I paid a visit to our mate at the undertaker's.'

'What happened?'

'Bit of a narrow escape... I got chased out the cemetery by these two gorillas in suits.'

'Death really brings out the worst in people,' said Frank as he pulled a threadbare jumper over his head.

'I see what you mean about the wires, do you know they move?'

Five shrugged. 'Tina reckons they are parts for tech competitions he enters.'

'You should see what they did to Granny Bamford, anyway why put them in a coffin?' Stubber lifted up Frank and plopped him into his wheelchair. 'It was all worth it though. I've got you all a lovely little present waiting downstairs.'

Ten minutes later there was a right old hoo-ha in the front room. Mags' knitting was being trampled mercilessly as everyone jostled for a place around the coffee table. It was as if some rare religious artefact was being unveiled. A closer inspection revealed something far more precious: the gloriously sparkling perfection of what goes by the name of a Moog synthesizer.

'Is it a loaner?' asked Don.

Stubber wagged his hands and wrinkled up his face, 'a kind of... permanent loan.'

Mags stared wide-eyed at the myriad switches and buttons. 'How the hell am I gonna work that lot out?'

'You should have a gander on Your Tube,' said Frank before ramming a mince pie in his mouth.

Five threw his arms around the huddled bodies 'This is the missing piece of the jigsaw, everyone.'

'You what?' said Stubber.

'I wasn't gonna bring it up today, but I've been talking with Don and we think it's time to take the next step.'

'Split up?' asked Frank, widening his eyes.

'Bombers Mark 2. We'll still be heavily influenced by Numan but we'll start doing our own stuff.'

'The phoenix rising from the ashes,' said Don closing his eyes and nodding gently to himself.

'Fucking yes!' Stubber punched the air. 'How long have I been waiting for this! What kinda stuff?'

Five paused and looked over at Don. 'The stuff we've been writing is like nothing else before it, a radical, dark-wave, hard-core, label-free, boundary breaking, progressive alternative.'

'It's the fucking future,' said Stubber loading up his vaporiser with a Christmas-themed mince pie flavoured e-liquid.

'Some of the lyrics that have been flowing out of me are just wild,' said Five, tapping at the notepad in his trouser pocket.

Stubber, growing increasingly animated, pointed to the equipment set-up in the conservatory. 'Play something.'

'We're still working on the music, but I can read you some lyrics.' To the accompaniment of the faint pattering of rain on the conservatory roof, Five looked around the room, staring coolly into everyone's eyes before clearing his throat. 'This is a song called… The Clones.'

Five was about to begin his profound rendition when he was halted by a banging noise from the other side of the house.

'What the hell is that?' He walked out into the hallway toward a muffled noise emanating from the direction of his bedroom. After conducting a very brief investigation, he returned to the front room with eyes as wide as bass drums. 'Does anyone happen to know why my old geography teacher is duct-taped to the chair in my bedroom?'

Stubber rubbed the back of his neck. 'Oh… yeah… I was about to—'

'Only if it's no trouble.'

'I've been having difficulty accepting what happened the other night—'

'Haven't we all, but you can't go around kidnapping people!' said Mags, hobbling across the room.

'That's a strong word. I've borrowed him for a few hours, I just wanted to set up a parley.'

'You've been watching *The Sopranos* again haven't you?' said Frank.

'Why couldn't you arrange to meet him in a cafe?' said Five.

'Yeah, like he'd agree to that!'

Mags pointed at Stubber. 'You've got five minutes to get him out of *this* house before I call the Old Bill.' She picked her mobile phone off the sideboard and hobbled off to the kitchen.

No one was willing to bet that Mags wouldn't honour that threat, so Five and Stubber quickly relocated themselves to the bedroom to tend to the tied up tyrant.

The strangest of circumstances in life can often teach us the strangest of things. It turns out that the best way to dismantle a finely-tuned waxed moustache is to rip a ten centimetre length of gaffer tape off it at high speed. Mr Morris yelped as a line of drool leapt off his chin and into the biscuit crumb and tobacco exhibit that decorated the lapels of his smoking jacket.

'How dare you—'

'Put a sock in it,' growled Stubber.

'I'll be contacting the authorities, this is an outrage!'

''Ow about I rip your nuts off?' Stubber twisted Mr Morris's ear until it folded in on itself.

'Arhh!'

Unsure how to play this rather bizarre set of cards he'd been dealt, Five began by placing his hand on Stubber's shoulder to placate him. He then stared down at old shitpits whose head was as red as boiling magma and whose eyes looked ready to pop out of his skull. *What the hell am I going to do? Call the police and deny any part in it? Surely I'd be blamed anyway?* Maybe this was best viewed as an opportunity. A chance to make a few corrections. But would it be right to take advantage of this situation? Who was qualified to say? Some believe that two wrongs don't make a right, while others think the end justifies the means. He would have to worry about the ethical incongruities another day; after all, morality can be such a messy business.

'Our problem,' said Five, 'is that we think our band weren't given a fair roll of the dice.'

'The dice have always been loaded against *you* boy.'

'There's no way you were an impartial judge and there was also no way we should have lost.'

'But you did.'

'It wasn't fair, though.'

'Life *rarely* is.'

'So why not do something to correct that?'

'Never.' Mr Morris jerked his head sideways in a show of defiance.

'So, you're happy for me to let Stubsy take you for a little trip into the woods in his van?'

'That lumbering oaf doesn't scare me.'

'What will you do with him Stubsy?'

'Vat of acid,' he answered, a bit too quickly.

'You have neither the guts nor the gumption.' Mr Morris glared at Stubber from beneath his bushy eyebrows.

This wasn't working and Stubber had a certain glint in his eye that always worried Five. Hopefully these were only scare tactics. He could hear his mum shuffling about in the hallway near to where the telephone was. He knew he didn't have long. He needed a new angle and fast. He could have done with some of Pete's lateral thinking. *Pete, yes of course. You genius!*

Five bent down as close as he could bear to Mr Morris' hairy ear hole and spoke calmly and quickly.

'There are two ways we can play this. The first, you help us. The second, you go to the police and I ask Stubsy to pay a visit to Mr Pinner, our contact at *The Romford Gazette*. He loves a bit of salacious gossip and I'm sure Stubsy can convince him to run an article.'

'You've got *nothing* on me.'

Five smiled and played his trump card. 'Only that... my best mate Pete Hampton had a drug-fuelled threesome with the tournament judge Mr West *and* his wife. Who's to say you weren't involved?'

'That's extortion!'

'The *Gazette* would have a field day,' said Stubber. 'Imagine the headline, "Nazi geography teacher in psychedelic four-way bi-love romp with ex-pupil".'

'Imagine how that would go down with the teachers' union?' said Five. 'That stuff tends to stick, you can trust me on that.'

'I'm retiring next year,' said Mr Morris looking up at Stubber, the colour draining from his face. 'You wouldn't dare.'

Stubber nodded theatrically. 'Trust me mate, nothing would make me happier.'

Mr Morris dropped his shoulders and hung his head. 'What do I have to do?'

22

THE STATE OF THINGS TO COME

25th December

Amass of wires crashed against the wall and landed on the dust-laden floorboards. Tina stood close to the door; her calves twitched as they stiffened.

'Fucking little shit.'

'Is this really helping?'

'It's my neck on the line, not yours.'

She took a deep breath to steady her voice. 'He's many things, but no thief.'

Ross swept his arm across the work bench sending tools and machine parts clattering about Tina's feet. 'Can you believe it? He smuggled it out of here in a coffin and completely hijacked Granny Bamford's funeral!'

'You're joking?'

'Does it look like it? I've had to put her back on ice. Do you know how much that costs? She's not embalmed, you know, not with the price they paid.' He slammed down another synthesizer that looked like it was only half built. 'I'll never get this ready in time, he's trying to get his own back I reckon.'

'Could you blame him?'

'On his side now, are you?'

No reply.

'I'm telling you *he* nicked that synth.'

'He's no capable.'

'Same old story.' He ripped out a circuit board and threw it over his shoulder. 'No one *ever* believes me.'

'Why is that synth so important?'

'I had just fixed it for Numan and he needs it back for a gig he's got *this* weekend.'

'Can't you buy him a new one?'

He stopped, head tilted, piercing her with his protruding eyes. 'It *has* to be that one.'

'Why?'

'Why so many fucking questions?'

'Wouldn't it be kinder to know for sure if he did this, before you start making threats?'

'Is that all you bleeding-heart liberals care about, "kindness"?'

'You make it sound like a curse.'

'Do you know what people do when you're kind to them?'

She jolted her right shoulder in an uncommitted half-shrug. A clear act of aggression that had Ross stabbing his synthesizer with uncontrolled jolts of his screwdriver. Bits of processing board splintered onto his work bench.

Tina stepped backwards, placing herself in the mouth of the door.

'...they fucking walk all over you.'

She raised her eyebrows and threw her handbag over her shoulder. Outside, the shrill tones of a police siren came and went down the high street.

'What, even on Christmas Day?'

'It'll be our last one, if I don't think of something.'

'What the hell are you talking about?'

'You want to do something important with your life, something your dad would have been proud of?'

'Aye, you know I do.'

'Then you need to forget about "kindness" darling, that never won any wars.'

'Maybe not, but we're not at war.'

'Really?' Ross lifted the synth over his head and smashed it into the floor. 'You haven't got a clue what's coming have you?'

Tina stayed mute, staring at the floor for fear of making the situation worse. Ross trampled over the splintered machine parts and grabbed his trench coat off the back of the door. 'That little bastard is gonna pay for this.' He pushed past Tina and stormed out. 'You can let yourself out.'

Tina waited for the sound of the hearse as it left the fore-court, then as she was walking over to his desk to turn off the lamp something caught her eye. Ross's laptop had been left on with his email account open. It was staring up at her, almost inviting her to look. She knew she shouldn't. What if Dad was looking down on her? What if she got caught? She pulled up a chair, sat down and started reading.

23

BABYLON'S BURNING

28th December

Not being late for your appointment helps, but they still expect blood. Or as they put it, "prove you are actively seeking employment". They make you write down what websites you've been looking at – like Pete was going to do that! He sat down at the benefit officer's desk, feeling – as he usually did – a volatile blend of vulnerable dependency and principled repugnance.

'Good morning Mr Hampton, I hope you had a pleasant Christmas? Do you have the list of jobs you have applied for?' The officer's gaze was glued to his computer screen as if under a wizard's spell. His desk was spotless, shiny and clutter-free save for a solitary wooden framed picture of himself standing proudly next to a Jaguar E-Type classic sports car.

'Have we been transported to Rivendell, brother?'

'Excuse me?'

'Where are all these mythical jobs you speak of?'

'You mean you haven't applied for *anything*?'

NICKY BLUE

'I've been so caught up with actively seeking employment, I haven't had time.' Pete grinned.

A tremor registered on the officer's chin. 'There are *plenty* of jobs out there if you are prepared to be' – he turned his computer screen around to face Pete – 'a little more flexible.'

Pete moved in close to the screen and squinted. 'A shelf-stacker in a fucking pound shop? The exploitation of the third world to allow the privileged few to destroy the planet with cheap plastic novelty shit?!'

The officer adjusted his tie and sighed heavily. 'Maybe we need to look at your transferable skills again. It says here you are interested in academia?'

Pete thrust a solitary fist into the air. 'I want to teach the people how to dismantle patriarchy.'

'But you don't have any formal teaching qualifications. Have you ever considered working in a call centre? It's very sociable.'

'It would be doomed to failure brother, I'm intrinsically anti-social.' Pete sucked air in through his gappy teeth whilst tapping his fingers on the edge of the desk. 'I write anarchic poetry… maybe I could apply to become the poet laureate?'

'There's no category on the computer for that I'm afraid.' The officer's limp hands prodded absently at his keyboard. It was almost as if his heart wasn't in it. 'The closest we have is a position – just in today – for a cleaner at the library. Can I put you forward for that?'

'No, I don't think so.'

'Why don't you just go for the interview experience?'

'Absolutely not brother.' Pete reached down for one of the keys attached to the chain on his belt and used it to dig grime from under his thumb nail.

'I have to tell you Mr Hampton, if you continue to take this obstructive attitude to employment possibilities, I'll be forced to apply a benefit sanction. I've given you too many chances already.' The officer, now beetroot-faced, attempted to assert himself whilst keeping his eyes transfixed to his screen.

'Hey, I'm trying my best here.' Pete sat erect on the edge of his seat.

'I don't think you're taking this very seriously.'

'Because I don't fit in with your version of reality?'

'There's only one reality.' The officer's eyes widened as if surprised by his own comment.

'So, you're coaching me on metaphysics now?'

These were unchartered waters for a benefits officer; the Jobcentre had offered him nothing in the way of training on how to deal with the challenges of philosophical debate. 'Erm... I meant there's only one job market.'

'…. Yeah, full of shitty jobs no one wants to do.'

'*Somebody* has to do them.'

Unable to hold himself down a second longer, Pete leapt to his feet, pushed the computer screen to the other side of the desk and bent forward to stare into the officer's face. 'Can I ask you a question, brother?'

'Wh-what would that be?' the officer blinked rapidly at the intrusion.

'Are you happy in your job?'

'… It pays the mortgage.'

'It's sucking every ounce of love from your soul though isn't it?'

The officer swallowed hard. 'I… really don't know what you're talking about.'

Pete's attention was diverted by his phone vibrating. He looked down to see a text from his mum: 'Three men in the garden, come quick.' He grabbed his rucksack and sprinted towards the door, shouting back at the officer over his shoulder, 'I'm sorry to have to do this to you brother but I'm putting you on a work sanction. I forbid you to carry out any form of employment that doesn't fill your heart with joy and wonder. I will expect a full report on my next visit.'

As he careered out of the building (so to speak) he found himself spinning across a glacial pavement. It was at that moment the world went Pete Tong – a misty flash of green hair; the pages of the Anarchist Federation magazine flapping through the bitter air like a baby dragon; three pounds and twenty-eight pence in change cascading from a pocket like a penny falls arcade game. Then there was a short-long in-between moment of fuzzy nothingness accompanied by a sharp spasm in the back of the throat, both of which were rudely interrupted by the cracking sound of spinal bone on tarmac. Lying winded in the gutter, Pete pushed himself up into a sitting position, whipped his mask off and regurgitated the previous evening's chickpea curry into his lap. Say what you will, Pete was always a class act. You can't teach it, you can't learn it. In any case, he was in no state of mind to let a minor mishap like this hinder him in any way, so he hurriedly set about weighing up his options for getting home as quickly as possible: 1. wait for a bus (time to reach home in rush hour, approximately forty minutes); 2. get a taxi – not an option, he only had three pounds and twenty-eight pence, most of which had gone down the drain; 3. run and risk almost certain death on these pavements, unless…

'Get out the fucking road you lunatic!' an irate driver leaned out of his window to scream at Pete, who had decided that the safest and quickest way to run home was down the middle of the road. An act which he carried out with scant regard for the trail of honking cars and abusive threats in his wake. His bandy legs carried him all the way down the High Street, across the roundabout, and then a short cut through Cottons Park which backed onto his mum's house. His tatty old army boots dug into the soles of his feet as he ran, causing a searing pain he had no choice but to ignore. He yanked his phone out of his pocket and hit speed dial.

'Hello… Pete?' Five answered the call sounding extremely distressed.

'Brother… you've got… to get… everyone out the house.' Pete stopped to lean against a tree and gather his breath. 'They are closing in… no time to explain… trust me.'

'We're all at the hospital, Don's collapsed… I'm so scared, what's happening?'

'I'll be there… soon as I can.' Pete got himself moving again. He took a short cut through a dense cluster of trees. As he got closer to his mum's back garden he hit an acrid fog of thick black smoke. He pulled up his face mask and pressed down hard on it until he cleared the trees. It was then he saw the high-definition horror of fifty-foot flames raging from the roof of his mobile home. Debris danced on the foggy haze surrounding the furnace and the loud crackling sound of heat devouring timber reverberated like the sound of hell itself. Pete's only thought was for his mum. He kicked open the gate and searched for a way past the fire to reach her bunga-low. His only option was a tight gap between his mobile home and next door's fence, both of which had turned the gap into a corridor of fire. Pete unzipped his rucksack and, pulling it over his head, ran blindly through the flames. He was almost clear when a gas bottle exploded, flinging him into the fence and then down onto his mum's rose bushes where he lay draped, twisted and motionless like a discarded rag doll.

24

EVERYTHING TO LOSE

31st December - New Year's Eve

If one looks closely enough, art can be seen in the most unlikely of places. Take, for example, sunlight pouring through half-open blinds, casting velveteen brush strokes on an unmade bed. The exhibit I'm referring to was definitely more Jackson Pollock than Rembrandt, though it was conceptually boosted by a third dimension of sound. Discordant trolley wheels, hurried footsteps and intercoms all colliding chaotically in the hospital corridor outside Don's room.

Nurse Kelly was a chirpy middle-aged woman who, as a result of having orders barked at her from pompous consultants for the past thirty years, was more than a little sympathetic to the pair of incapacitated revolutionaries she was tending to.

'You mean take up arms against the state and force everyone to meditate?'

'That's the question.' The slow click of Don's prayer beads was just audible beneath the beep of the heart monitor resonating against the bare walls of the cardiology ward. 'Can one wrong deed be justified in the pursuit of a greater happiness?'

'Of course it can brother.' Pete had skipped the burns unit and made himself a nest consisting of two plastic chairs and eight tasteful pink hospital blankets he'd managed to blag off the nurse as the result of some heavy flirting. Pete's right leg, having taken the majority of the blast, was swaddled in bandages and – having been ordered to keep it upright – was propped on the edge of Don's bed. He had told Don his gas heater exploded. Sure, it was untrue, but it perfectly illustrated the point in question.

'People would likely die, though?' said Don, clearly uneasy at the suggestion.

'Thousands are being slaughtered for lesser causes every day,' Pete quickly countered.

'A doctor died here in the hospital, last Tuesday,' said Kelly joining in, 'he tripped and fell down the staircase.'

'Sorry to hear that.' Don placed his palm at his heart.

'Apparently he'd seen a pop star and was after his autograph.'

'Who was it?' asked Pete

'H from Steps.'

Pete frowned, 'the tragic irony.'

'I know, he doesn't give autographs apparently.' The nurse flapped a clean blanket over Don.

A junior doctor scurried into the room. Hair erupted from his scalp like a wild rhododendron, though its spectacle was only partially successful in distracting one from his glazed expression. He picked up the clipboard hanging from the end of Don's bed and screwed up his eyes like a midnight drunk trying to read a bus timetable. After tutting a few times to himself he turned to Kelly. 'We need to run some more tests, nurse. Can we prep for an exercise thallium scan in thirty minutes?'

Kelly nodded.

The doctor then peered over in Pete's direction. 'Shouldn't you be in bed too?'

Pete winked at him. 'That depends, do you fancy tucking me in?'

Kelly covered her mouth to stifle her laugh.

The doctor stared hard at Pete for a moment before tutting again and leaving the room.

With the coast clear, Kelly burst out laughing. 'Did you see his face? Priceless! Do you know he's never even asked me my name?'

'He's gagging for it,' said Pete. 'I rarely misread signals like that.'

'You're a naughty boy aren't you?' said Kelly with a glint in her eye. 'Anyway I better do as the master orders.' Kelly picked up her supply bag and left the room.

It wasn't long before the unmistakable squeak of Frank's rusty wheelchair could be heard rattling down the corridor. Five and Frank had gone on ahead while Mags went in search of a consultant. Don had been in for two days now and they still hadn't been given any solid information on his condition. Five had been climbing the walls; even higher than usual.

'Pete, what the hell happened?'

Pete looked up at Frank and then toward Five. 'We're gonna have to tell them soon.'

'Tell us what?' said Frank

'Three blokes smashed up my place and set fire to it.'

'Three?' Five grabbed the crease in his arm.

'The police found Mum locked in the pantry, she was bricking it but she escaped the fire, thank fuck. She's gone to stay with my auntie until we can sort this.'

'Who the hell would do that?' Frank dug around in his wheelchair for his tobacco pouch.

'Mum didn't get a good look but I know this is the work of Ross. I'm certain he's a government agent leading some high-level alien conspiracy investigation. It's not safe for any of us to go home.'

Frank dropped his pouch and covered his legs in tobacco.

'That's what *you* think,' said Five.

'I intercepted another email since I've been in here. Ross was kicking off about a device that was in one of his synths that got stolen. Something called an "Interplantery Signal Blocker" – still think he's an undercover immigration officer?'

Five shrugged, 'It's no worse than your theory.'

'Why would immigration officers want us dead?'

'What about that cheap baccy you all smuggled back?' said Frank scraping up his own and dropping it into a Rizla on his lap.

'That was 1985,' said Pete, 'it wasn't frowned upon then.'

Don buckled forward, letting out a series of short wheezes.

Five leapt to his bedside. 'Are you OK?'

'Yeah... don't worry... I'm fine.'

Five reached over the bed to press the call button but Don grabbed his hand. 'Don't... she'll be back soon anyway.' Don took some deep breaths and sat upright again. 'It's been happening since I collapsed. One minute I was giving Mum a demo on the new synth, the next thing I was on the floor. My heart stopped for three minutes apparently.... I nearly migrated to the other side.' Don smiled through his grimace and pointed up toward a transcendental gateway in the ether. It's always useful to know where to find it.

Five stared at the mass of pads and wiring attached to his brother's chest and followed them up to the heart monitor beeping irregularly, his furrowed brow just visible under his baseball cap. 'Where's that bloody nurse got to?'

'Whatever this business is,' said Frank, 'I think you should take everything you know to the police.'

'Agreed,' said Five.

'That's the worst idea in the world,' said Pete rolling to

one side and yanking the hospital gown out of his butt. 'They could be involved—'

'Well I'm doing it—' snapped Five.

'We're so close, we just need to find the truth.'

'Everyone's obsessed with the bloody truth.'

'Give me two days.'

Five walked over to the window and peered through the blinds, trying to gather his thoughts. 'Twenty-four hours. We can find a B & B for tonight then we're going home.'

The doctor came hurtling back into the room clutching a cup of coffee, with nurse Kelly in tow. He picked up the clipboard again and muttered something to Kelly who promptly walked over to the monitor and pressed some buttons that made it sound like R2D2.

Five looked up at the unintelligible graphs flickering across the screen. He could feel his shoulders tighten and his jaw clench. 'Doctor, we really need answers.'

The doctor, trying to focus on the clipboard again, 'His heart beat is still irregular.'

'I thought that was what the pacemaker was for?'

'It was.' The monitor made a series of prolonged beeps that grabbed the doctor's attention.

'Why isn't it working then?'

'We don't know… we need to run more tests.'

'When are you going to do that?'

'Now, if you'll let me.' The doctor looked up at the clock above Don's bed. 'Visiting hours are over anyway. I'm going to have to ask you all to leave.' He then turned and pointed to Pete. 'That includes you, I need you to return to your own ward.'

'What happens if I don't?' Pete stuck his nose in the air.

'You have to.' The doctor's eyebrows disappeared into the anarchy of his unkempt hair.

'I don't.'

'You must.'

'I won't.'

'You will.'

'I won't.'

'Then I will be forced to call security.'

'Gimme a kiss and I'll go.'

'*Absolutely* not.' The doctor's posture stiffened.

'How about a little cuddle?'

This time, Kelly couldn't stop herself laughing.

'This is *completely* inappropriate.'

'You're not homophobic are you doctor?' Kelly couldn't resist.

'Of course not.' The doctor's face flushed pink.

'Come and prove it then.'

Five walked over to stand in front of Pete and, grabbing his head between his hands, 'Can you for once just shut the fuck up?'

'Unbelievable,' said the doctor shaking his head. 'You try and do your best for people.'

'I'm very sorry doctor, he doesn't mean it—'

Pete's head popped out from behind Five, 'I bloody well do.'

The doctor dropped his clipboard, 'I'm sick of this…'

The heart monitor beeped again, this time a louder, higher pitched sound. Kelly's smile had fallen away and she was frantically pressing buttons on the monitor. 'Doctor can you come and look at this please.'

'I'm sick of working eighty-hour weeks,' continued the doctor, 'of never seeing my kids, the constant lack of sleep, the shit canteen food… but worst of all is having to listen to whining little maggots like you.'

'Doctor, now please,' repeated Kelly.

Undeterred, Pete pushed Five aside, 'You're not the only one that goes without sleep brother, I do all-nighters all the time—'

The beeps got even louder. Kelly ran across the room and dragged on the doctor's sleeve.

'Yes but I'm here trying to save lives, you're probably looking at porn, you waster!'

Desperate, Five put his hand over Pete's mouth and pushed hard to subdue the tirade of expletives.

Don crumpled forward, gasping for oxygen.

Kelly, still unable to get a coherent response from the doctor, slapped him round the face, 'Fucking do something!'

Red lights flashed on the monitor and a piercing alarm sounded in the corridor. Another nurse ran into the room. The beeping had now turned to a constant drone, a flatline. The nurse kicked the locks of the bed's wheels, 'We need to get him to intensive care now.'

At last the doctor snapped out of his rage and joined the two nurses in gathering behind the bed as it was hurriedly pushed from the room.

'Please wait here,' Kelly shouted to Five as she left the room. 'I'll be back as soon as I can.'

With that, Don's bed disappeared.

The monitor screeched for another thirty seconds before subsiding into ghostly silence.

The room was calm again, save for hostile glares fixed on Pete.

Pete dared not look up from the floor.

Before anyone could speak, Mags had entered the room. 'Where's Don?'

DEAR GARY

There's some pretty heavy shit going on. I'm not sure exactly what is happening but there's a chance it involves your keyboard technician Ross Patterson. I know it might seem that I'm trying to discredit him but I don't think he is who he says he is. Also I'm not sure if you heard about what happened at battle of the bands last week? He pretty much sabotaged the whole gig. He's a nasty bit of work. I just wanted to warn you.

Five
P.S. My brother Don is in hospital with heart problems. I'm petrified of losing him.

25
WHAT WE DARE NOT MENTION

January the 7ᵗʰ, 11 am

Who are you?
Looming phantom,
Made of voodoo,
I hear you creeping down the hallway…
Bleeding tiny embers,
BOO!

I f your life isn't quite as fucked up as you had hoped for, it's never too late to try therapy. Five's next appointment with Mrs Summerisle had come at a time when he felt 'mitigating circumstances' should dictate he'd be excused from attending. Mags failed to agree. Luckily, the therapy service was only a short walk from the bus stop, yet just long enough for the cold to penetrate deep into his bones. He dragged himself past the industrial estate, moving as if he was wearing chain mail. Above him, the cranes stood taller than ever, huddled together like gatekeepers of the underworld; scheming the apocalypse.

'Good to see you again, Five. How have you been?'

Five waggled his frostbitten hand. 'Up and down.'

'Did you remember to bring your diary?'

Five cleared his throat and crossed his arms. 'No, I... forgot.'

Judy put her reading glasses on and stared down at her notes, nodding to herself, 'hmm.' She sunk her hand into the back of her frizzy mop and scratched hard. Her nails causing a rasping sound on her dry scalp. *It must be at least fifty degrees in here.* Five was forced to take off his jacket, which he draped over the arm of his chair. Ready for a quick escape. Already his breath was growing shallow and a tingling unreality was setting in. *I'll just make an excuse... what can I say?*

What looked like the blackbird from his last visit reappeared at the window and tapped against it with his beak. Without breaking her gaze, Judy reached her arm behind her and pushed the window up wide enough for it to come inside.

Five pointed at the creature. 'Is that the same one as last time?'

Judy nodded. 'I call him Sigmund, I think he must have been a therapist in a former life. Or he's just here for the mealworms.'

'I think I have to leave.'

'Why?'

Just let me go.

'My brother is sick in hospital. I want to see him.'

'I'm very sorry to hear that, I hope it's not serious?'

'We don't know yet, it's heart related.'

Judy looked up at the clock on the wall. 'What time do visiting hours start?'

'Er... 3pm,' mumbled Five.

'It's only 11.10 now.'

'I've already told you this is not going to help,' tutted Five, grabbing hold of his jacket. 'Everyone seems to know what's best for me, like I just tell them what's wrong and I'm cured. Don't you think I would have done that by now if it was that easy?'

'Where's the harm in telling me then?'

'Telling you what?'

Judy looked down at her notes. 'You said there was an event?'

Five found the outcrop of flesh on the inside of his cheek again and started chewing.

If you think I'm spilling my guts, you can think again.

'I'm too worried about Don at the moment.' Five rubbed at his watery eyes, smearing eyeliner across his pale skin.

'This is an opportunity for *you*.'

'NO! I can't…' He lent forward, straining for air. The metallic taste of blood registering at the base of his tongue.

Breathe, breathe.

'Doesn't everyone have something they are too scared to think about?'

Judy gave him a short, gentle smile. A register of compassion without letting him wriggle free.

Sigmund teetered on the window frame, looking unsure about coming inside. Eyes darting frantically.

Five pulled his coat over his lap and sunk his nails into his arm.

'What's the worst that will happen?'

Looking out of the window, a grey murky sky offered Five no clues as to his next move. He had been a prisoner to this for so long. He was exhausted. How much longer could he…? Then, a moment of surrender.

'They… could come back.'

'Who?'

'I didn't see who they were… they had ski masks on.' Five

felt the tears running down his cheeks.

Judy handed him a glass of water which he gulped down. Its coolness momentarily calmed the fire in his nervous system.

'What happened?'

'I was walking back from my friend Pete's one night… these three guys grabbed me and forced me into the boot of their car… they drove me out into Hainault forest… they took it in turns to beat the shit out of me… they kept checking my body for – things, I don't know what… they said they would kill me if I told anyone. I was found the next day by a man walking his dog… I was in hospital for a month.'

'Did you go to the police?'

'I was too scared, I told everyone it was a paragliding injury, I only ever told Tina the truth.'

Sigmund jumped down from the window ledge onto Judy's desk and picked up a big mealworm in its beak.

'I can't imagine how terrifying that must have been for you.'

'How terrifying it still is…'

'Excuse me?'

'I think they are back.' Five felt his pulse quicken further. 'My best mate Pete had his place burnt down by three guys. I don't know for sure as Pete has pissed so many people off. One thing's for certain though, I need to look after my family.'

Having swallowed his worm, Sigmund – now looking pleased with himself – hopped back up onto the window ledge and fluttered away into the Romford sky.

Cotton Park was directly across the road from the therapy service. It was the perfect place for Five to try and clear his head. He walked down the steps and made his way over to the jetty on the boating lake. Stepping onto the slimy wooden decking, he carefully navigated the journey to the end, where he crouched down and took a deep breath in. One of his earliest memories was of the time when Frank used to bring him and Don here in the summer holidays. The sunlight used to glimmer off the water as they raced the peddle boats to the other side. Today the wind blew jagged ripples across the lake's surface. Five stared down at his distorted reflection.

Five looked at his phone. It was time to go home and prepare some lunch before they all set off to visit Don. As he turned to leave, he noticed someone on the other side of lake. It was the old lady that had been following him. Her face looked disjointed yet somehow familiar. Being out in the open, this was maybe his chance to get to her before she disappeared again. He jumped to his feet, forgetting how slippery the decking was. After no more than a couple of steps, he lost his footing and tumbled from the jetty into the icy water.

The shock
The absence
The reeds upon the skin
Tightening
Ice demons tip toe down the spine.
The bitter, bitter sting

So beautifully broken
By the weight of it all
Dragging downward
One final glance upwards, towards the fading light.

The old lady.

Then… nothing.

NUMAN AND THE MACHINE

7th January

The call of the great horned owl could be heard in the trees adjacent to the great arching stained glass windows of the spire. It was carried on the breeze that dipped and swirled through the dusty Hollywood Hills. Beneath it, numerous little legs scurried through the undergrowth and huddled under a vast bronze dragon that guarded the mansion gates. It was one of those full moon nights where everything alive was awake. Inside the spire, the moonlight shimmered off a gilded mirror that hung upon the cool stone wall, barely revealing the outline of the figure lying on the floor in front of it. Gary Numan had been inputting random binary digits late into the night, driven by an overwhelming compulsion to succeed at any cost. The object of his obsession was a small gold box – no bigger than a Rubik's Cube – plain, save for the two buttons 0 and 1 embedded into its lid. He muttered incessantly under his breath while he jabbed at the buttons. With the gig coming up at the Royal Albert Hall, his

223

list of jobs was enormous and this was taking up far too much of his time. If it wasn't for Brewis he wouldn't have a chance of completing even half of his chores. He paused and stared down at the box whilst gritting his teeth. Was anything ever going to come of this? He continued for a few more moments before letting out a scream – 'Ahh!' – and with that he slapped the box across the floor. He rose up vertically and shouted down into the dark bowels of the tower, 'Brewis!'

No reply

'Brewis… BREWIS.'

The slow hollow clang of boots on metal echoed up the spiral staircase until a weary face appeared in the doorway. Dark crescents hung down under his swollen eyes. He reached out to support himself on the door frame whilst panting heavily. He can't have been any more than in his mid-thirties but his upper torso was so twisted and curled he gave the appearance of a much older man.

'I've been calling you!'

'I'm sorry M—'

'I don't want your excuses.'

'The toilets are blocked again M—'

'It's always the toilets, isn't it?'

Brewis stayed mute, hunched forward as if suspended by an invisible meat hook.

'I need you to compose a letter for me.'

Brewis dug a small pad of paper from his ripped overalls and hobbled over to the window so he could work in the moonlight. His shadow stretched back across the room like a varicose vein as he waited patiently for Gary to speak.

Mr R. Patterson
Wright-Patterson Funeral Directors
High Street
Romford

RM1 1AN
England.

Dear Ross,

I hope this letter finds you well. Following our latest band and management meeting, we have decided that, as a result of the current difficulties, we have taken the decision to change our keyboard technician. If you have any of our equipment still in your possession, could you please return it immediately. I would like to thank you for all your hard work and on behalf of the band and myself would like to wish you the very best for the future.

Yours sincerely,

Gary Numan.

ARE YOU WITH ME?

Ross
He's sacked me 18:08

Withheld
It doesn't matter, the orders are to stand down 18:11

Ross
With what we know? How can we do that? 18:12

Withheld
They don't want a scandal this close to an election 10:13

Five
Fuck that, It's time to stand up and be counted, before its too
late 10:15

Withheld
Do you mean what I think you do? 18:11

Ross
There's no other way. Are you with me? 18:12

Withheld
Yes 10:13

27

ZEBEDEE AND THE GHOST

January, 8.30 am

Pete rolled over on the bare mattress, unzipped his sleeping bag and opened his laptop. The surrounding floorboards were a mosaic of pizza boxes and crushed cider cans. He never thought he would find himself in a squat again. His leg, still bandaged and raw as hell, had throbbed through most of the night, keeping him awake. The painkillers helped a bit but he was running out fast and thought it too risky to leave the building during daylight hours. A notification popped up on his desktop: *Message from Ghost Hunter.*

Dear Z,

You are right, it wasn't easy getting in, but there's normally one glitch you can exploit.

Decoded and attached.

Fight the power

G.H.

2 8

ROGUE JUAN

January, 2.15 pm

Those numerous failed attempts at ridding mould from the ceiling were instantly recognisable. The sight of the jagged swirls in fading paint work afforded an unlikely comfort, in that they brought about two very welcome realisations. Five was at home and he was still alive. The wind whistled hard through his warped window frame. A storm was brewing so he pulled the quilt up snuggly round his neck. Buzzing on the floor beside him sat Frank's little heater, trying to make a dent in the temperature. Through the mottled blur of slowly fading dreamscapes he sensed a presence in the room. He turned to see an animated throng of bodies jostling to get a good look at him.

'You alright love?' Mags' voice cracked as she placed a cup of tea (in his favourite mug) on his bedside cabinet.

'Who pulled me out?'

'I did,' from behind the bodies stepped the old lady from the lake.

'Whu—?'

Before he could get his words out, she had grabbed at the bottom of her neck and pulled upwards. A layer of silicone film came away in her hand as the prosthetic mask tore from her face. Before him stood a smiling middle-aged woman with grey unkempt hair and a deep furrow that connected two thinning eyebrows.

'Bloody hell!' Frank's dentures dislodged and dangled precariously from the precipice of his gummy mouth.

Blinking hard, Five scanned the room for clues he may have been still dreaming. *What the hell is happening?* Staring at the woman a few moments longer, there was something familiar about her green eyes. Could it be? *Of course.* 'Jenny!… I thought you were—'

'Don's being discharged this afternoon,' Mags interrupted, 'he's going to be alright.'

'Thank God.' Five put a hand on his chest and sighed deeply, unable to take his eyes off Jenny.

'It was just a glitch with his pacemaker,' added Frank, trying to get around Stubber's tree trunk legs in his wheelchair.

Eagerly waiting in the wings was a certain Pete Hampton. 'I think I know why it happened brother, remember I told you about the Interplanetary Signal Blocker in the email I intercepted? It was designed to disrupt particular circuitry. It was in the keyboard Stubber nicked—'

'That's slander,' growled Stubber as he plugged his vaporiser into a wall. 'You been on all-nighter again, Spock?'

'—Don was playing it when he collapsed, wasn't he? Don't worry though, I just got it out of the synth and smashed it to pieces in the garden.'

'That synth better still bloody work.' Mags narrowed her eyes.

Five smiled and gently shook his head, 'It's good to see you mate.'

I think.

Pete tutted and skulked off to the rear of the room to submerge back into his virtual abyss.

'Mum, can you open the curtains please?'

'You… what love?' Mags almost tripped over herself as she shuffled to the window.

Sitting up and taking a sip of tea, Five beckoned Jenny to come join him on the bed. She sat down beside him and held his hand.

'So… the mask?'

'Sorry, I was planning on taking it off before you woke up.'

Five squinted and rubbed the back of his neck, his head still too foggy to order his thoughts.

Jenny's eyes welled up as she spoke. 'I thought I'd lost you yesterday.'

Five put down his tea and focused his gaze on a bare bit of wall directly in front of him. 'Something happened to me as I was sinking in that lake… I realised what I'd been missing… the reason why it's important to tell other people our fears… is about trusting them to witness our humanity. That's what heals us… it seems so obvious now.'

The room fell quiet, save for the rip of tissues and a soft whimper from Mags.

Pete scuttled back from his corner, 'I don't mean to spoil the love-in brother,' – he handed over his laptop – 'but this proves *everything* I've been gabbling on about.'

'What am I looking at?' Five scrabbled around on the bedside cabinet for his glasses.

'We've heard back from the Ghost Hunter, he's cracked the final encryption of the document. We've hit the mother-lode. Ross is an elite operative, one of three working for a secret offshoot of MI5 monitoring alien visitations.'

Five scrolled through the document, trying to focus on the myriad lines of fine print.

'Look what it says about the wires,' Pete pointed to a section at the bottom of the document. It read:

Warning, Reptilian Tube Technology, Do Not Engage, Keep Contained At All Times.

Stubber rolled his eyes and grabbed hold of Pete's arm, pulling him backwards. 'Come on rocket man, I think he needs to rest, don't you?'

Pete wriggled his bony arm, hopelessly trying to shake himself free of Stubber's iron grip. 'Haven't you got your Mensa group to go to?

'You what?' Stubber narrowed his eyes, unsure if he was having the piss taken out of him.

'They have to be the same three blokes that did my place,' Pete continued, 'can't you see that brother?'

Jenny snatched the laptop and started reading.

Five nodded at Pete. 'Remember when I was in hospital last year? It wasn't a paragliding accident, it was three blokes in balaclavas that kicked the shit out of me.'

A collective gasp reverberated through the room.

'See what I'm saying?' Pete wrestled free from Stubber and pointed at Five out of solidarity.

'I'm gonna pay that Ross a visit,' growled Stubber.

'He's up to something,' said Five, 'but alien visitations? He's obviously made that document up to make idiots out of us. He knew we'd try and dig the dirt up on him. If he's some alien hunter, why would he fix synths for Numan?'

Pete took up a position in front of the washing machine for maximum crowd exposure. 'Because. He's... an—'

'Quick as you like moonraker.' Stubber cracked his knuckles impatiently.

'—Alien. Quite an important one by all accounts.'

The room exploded in laughter. The only person not

laughing, apart from Pete, was Jenny, whose eyes remained transfixed to the laptop.

'Yeah' – said Stubber – 'cos if he was an alien the perfect way to hide it would be to start a band and sing about aliens. Comedy gold.'

'But that's the genius of it' – spluttered Pete – 'can't you see? he's hiding in plain sight.'

'Like Harold Shipman,' said Mags, looking at Frank.

'Was he an alien?' asked Frank, tilting his head to the side.

'Think about it.' Pete put his hands in prayer position and waggled them purposefully. 'Who would suspect him?'

'MI5?' grinned Stubber, looking pleased with himself.

Jenny slammed the laptop shut. 'What if it is true?' She swept her hair back off her forehead, which instantly fell back in wispy strands. 'Do you want to know why I stopped going out?'

All the heads in the room nodded. They had been debating this topic for the last five years.

'Numan had hired me for a few shows in 2015. We were playing the Royal Festival Hall and I was due to go to Gary's dressing room to do his makeup. When I walked in, there were three men in suits ransacking the place. I thought they were security to start with, but they pinned me to the floor and bombarded me with all these weird questions. How long had I worked for Gary? Had I witnessed anything strange about him? Had I seen any Numan fans acting suspiciously? They said they'd kill me if I told anyone about them, so I just went home and hid myself away. I figured if I pretended I'd lost my mind I'd be safe – who listens to the ramblings of a mad old woman?' She took hold of Five's hand again and squeezed as hard as she could. 'I was worried they'd come for you, so I used the mask to keep an eye on you.' Jenny buried her face in her hands. 'I failed you.'

Five lent forward and put his arms around her while the rest of the room looked like figures from a waxwork museum.

The tension was eventually dispersed by the tinny buzz of the doorbell. Frank wheeled himself off down the hallway, muttering to himself, 'I suspected all along…'

Pete had a victorious glint in his eye. 'The truth has prevailed, we can now—'

'Have you all lost your fackin' minds?' barked Stubber, before pausing to chug on his vaporiser. 'Do you really expect me to believe alien conspiracy stories from the ramblings of a space cadet and someone who looks like the girl from *The Exorcist* who grew up and lost her shit?' He turned to Jenny. 'No offence darlin'.'

'Listen to me instead then, you great lump.' Everyone turned around to see Tina in the doorway. She was looking flushed and breathless, clutching a handful of printed documents which she began handing around the room.

'These are some of Ross's emails showing he's part of some kind of elite taskforce, or at least was until this morning. I was just going to drop something off at the undertaker's when I heard Ross throwing things against the wall. He was in one of his rages again, so I hid in the vestibule and overheard a conversation between him and his two cronies. He said he'd been sacked by Numan and the department were closing his operation down. He's got this crazy notion that Numan is the spearhead of an imminent alien invasion. But here's the important bit: he's just found out Numan himself is flying into City Airport today with his band at 3.30pm.' Tina looked apprehensive. 'I think they're planning on taking him out.'

'Where to?' said Frank.

'No, OUT!' Tina ran a finger across her throat. 'He's gone rogue, they'll be leaving any time now and we've got to stop him.'

'Call the Old Bill,' said Mags.

'Aye, like they are going to believe us.'

'We've got to try,' said Jenny, fumbling in her bag, drawing out her phone and pounding at the screen.

'There's one more thing you need to know. The third guy with Ross and the Count is a Spanish bloke. I don't think he can speak English but from what I could make out he said he was bringing guns.'

Anxious glances dominoed around the room, coming to a grinding halt at Stubber who raised his chin and flexed his biceps in a gesture of defiance. It would take more than a shooter to take him down.

'What the fuck are we waiting for?' Five scrambled out of bed.

'You are going nowhere,' said Mags pointing at him. 'It's brass monkeys out there.'

'Sod that, this is Numan!' Five grabbed his combat trousers from the chair and pulled them on. 'He needs us.'

Stubber pulled his van keys out of his pocket. 'Maybe we can cut them off at the London Road roundabout. The traffic is dire today.'

'It's not safe,' said Mags, 'and we don't have the numbers.'

'Don't worry,' said Frank waving his hand in the air. 'I'll go.' He stuck a rollie in the corner of his mouth and wheeled himself towards the front door. 'Bagsy the front seat.'

'Well, we're all saved, what on earth was I worried about?'

Mags shook her head as the stomp of hurried feet followed her husband down the hallway.

29

ZOMBIE GRANDMA AND THE NEON DEATH WIRES

8th January, 3.05 pm

The sky over Romford was apocalyptic. Hailstones ricocheted against the windscreen as Stubber frantically revved his van into life. A thick fog of black smoke billowed from the exhaust pipe, matching the brooding clouds above. With only one barely serviceable wiper, visibility was, at best, poor. Jenny stayed behind to keep an eye on Mags, so that left Pete, Tina and Five to clamber into the back and huddle awkwardly on the war-torn mattress. The floor, having a thick film of oil, crisps and who-knows-what covering it - was best avoided.

'If we step on it we might be able to head him off at the roundabout.' Stubber pulled out onto the High Street and took a turbo-charged drag on his vaporiser. There's nothing like a good lung hit to get the adrenaline pumping.

'This reminds me of that film,' said Frank, grappling with his seat belt.

'Which one?'

'The one with the car chase…'

'Is that the one with that bloke in it?'

'Have you seen it?'

Stubber smiled to himself as he clicked into second gear. 'Eyes peeled everyone.'

'Your back windows are too dirty to see through,' said Tina.

'It's minging in here,' moaned Pete who was checking the satnav on his phone for the less congested routes to the airport.

'Keeps out prying eyes,' Stubber winked into the rear-view mirror. 'Know what I mean?'

A collective shudder ran through the van. Tina picked up her coat tails and folded them neatly into her lap.

The roundabout at the end of the High Street that joined the main A-roads was usually busy, but due to a fatal combination of roadworks and several half-price sales on at the shopping centre, today it was gridlocked. Stubber managed to squeeze the van through a gap to the edge of the large central island before grinding to a halt. The hail lashed down. Sharp tinny thuds on the roof echoed through the van. On the other side of the roundabout, on London Road, the blurred outline of a vehicle was trying to force a car from its path in order to get onto the central reservation. 'What's going on over there?' said Stubber.

Frank cranked himself forwards, pushing his face up against the windscreen to try and get a clearer view. 'I can't tell…it's too far.'

The vehicle's wheels screeched as it pushed the smaller car aside. The surrounding vehicle horns blared in disapproval and a siren sounded from somewhere behind them. Then, a flash of lightening and – just for a second – vision was restored. 'That's definitely a hearse!' said Frank, wobbling precariously on the edge of his seat. 'And it's got a flower wreath at the back that says GRAN.'

'Aye,' said Tina, 'that's your man.'

'I thought he was *your* man?' Five narrowed his eyes.

The hearse got free of the car and accelerated up the central reservation.

'He's getting away!' Frank peeled his face off the windscreen and gripped on tight to the roof handle.

'No he ain't,' said Stubber as he slammed a monkey's worth of designer cowboy boot to the floor, sending Five flying over Tina to land face-first into the mattress. This produced a facial skid-mark of smeared foundation. An action that had been replicated with sickening familiarity on the very same spot over the years. Knowing this, Tina hooked her arm around him to hoist him back up, prompting a buzzing sensation at the base of his amygdala which he wasn't sure how to interpret. It was either primal lust or travel sickness.

Stubber careered over the central island, the van rocking over the heaped flower beds. Following the path that had been cleared, Stubber got onto the reservation and set his sights on the hearse. He cranked the gear stick into fifth, causing the engine to roar then squeal as if having second thoughts. 'Come on baby, don't let me down now!'

Half a mile up the road and past the worst of the traffic, the hearse got back onto the motorway and disappeared up the fast lane.

'It's no good… he's too fast for me.'

'There's a short cut,' said Pete, expanding a section of map on his phone. 'Go left down the B177… it'll bring us out in Barking, we can make up ground there.'

Further down London Road – just before the junction at Chadwell Heath – Trevor and Lance Bamford were pacing up and down impatiently, outside the gates of the Tanera Mor funeral park. They had just ushered in all their family and friends, who had taken up their positions around a hole in the ground. They were understandably keen to ensure that the second attempt at giving their dear old mum a dignified send-off was a tad more successful than the first. The only thing preventing this from happening at present was the fact that the deceased herself had yet to arrive. To say the brothers were somewhat peeved to see their mother's hearse roaring past the cemetery at twice the speed limit would be, then, to utter a tsunami of understatement. Trevor was on the blower pronto.

''Ello? Mr Hampton?'

'Yeah?'

'You got lost or sumfing?'

'What?'

'I've just seen you driving past the cemetery.'

'Who's this?'

'Mr Bamford, the son of the lady you are supposed to be burying twenty minutes ago.'

'Shit! I forgot it was today.'

A heavy silence.

'Something's come up mate. Can I drop her off later?'

'You fackin' wot?'

'Wot's 'appening?' Lance was trying to listen in on the receiver.

'We've got 400 people, dripping wet and freezing to death here... what am I gonna tell my kid? Someone's nicked his fackin' granny?'

'You couldn't pick her up from the airport, could you?'

Lance grabbed the phone. 'Listen you muppet, if you haven't turned around in the next five seconds, I'll be burying two people today.'

The next sound to travel down the phone was the lonely 'burrr' of a dead line.

'He's only fackin' hung up— in the motor, NOW!'

screamed Lance, fumbling in his pocket for his car keys. 'He wasn't even wearing the top hat.'

Directly above North London, cruising at an altitude of 15,325 feet, Gary Numan strapped on his seat belt as his airplane started to descend. Next to him Brewis was bent forward, fast asleep. A thin line of saliva from the corner of his mouth stretched down, painting circles on the toes of his battered Doctor Martin boots.

'Ladies and gentlemen, we will soon be landing at London City Airport. The local time is 3.25pm and the temperature is three degrees celsius. We apologise for the turbulence experienced as a result of the stormy conditions. Please ensure your seat belt is securely fastened. It just remains for me to say, on behalf of Centauri Airlines, thank you for travelling with us today and we hope to welcome you on board again soon.'

Gary peered down at the winding serpent of the Thames as London slowly materialized through the murky clouds. Underneath his seat his briefcase began to make a sharp beeping sound. He hurriedly picked it up and took out his small gold box. The implications of this sound were nothing short of immense. The frequency of the sound quickened – becoming rhythmical – like a ship's sonar. This drew the attention of the air stewardess.

'Excuse me Mr Numan, if you wouldn't mind switching off all your electrical equipment, please?'

'Oh this is just a game,' Gary smiled and flicked his head back. 'A very frustrating game.'

The air stewardess nodded and, looking over her shoulder as she turned to leave, said, 'I couldn't trouble you for an autograph could I? My husband is a massive fan.'

Gary signed a napkin and then quickly typed a series of binary digits into the box. Through the aircraft's windows, the illuminated markings of the runway had come into view and the sharp whir of hydraulic pumps rang out as the landing gear descended. Gary pushed Brewis upright and then gripped hold of the arm rests to brace himself as the plane's wheels hit the tarmac with an eighty-ton thump.

It was 3.30pm by the time Stubber found the security gate at the western end of the airport. A tailback of traffic stretched the length of the car park and Ross was already at the front of the queue.

'This is a matter of international security,' said Ross waving an official looking ID at the perplexed security guard. 'I need access to the runway now.'

'Have you got an airside permit sir?' asked the guard.

He pushed his ID so close to the man's face it was almost touching his nose. 'This should be clearance enough.'

'We'll need MI6 verification, sir. We'll also need to check your vehicle and escort you onto the runway.'

'There's *no* time, let us in now.'

'I'm going to have to phone this upstairs, sir, I'm sorry.' The guard clicked his walkie talkie. 'Yes governor, we have a hearse down here—'

Ross took out his gun and placed it on the man's temple. 'Let us in NOW.'

The barrier sprung up and the vehicles in the queue poured past the checkpoint as the guard ran for help, shouting into his walkie talkie.

Ignoring the five miles-an-hour speed limit, Ross sped through the apron and past the planes parked nose-out from the departure lounge. He swerved on the wet tarmac, narrowly missing several ground staff unloading a luggage trolley. With the runway now in sight, he smashed through the final barrier and skidded onto the outer landing strip. Not far behind, the Bamford boys had broken free from the queue and were hurtling after him. The response from airport security was instant. The flashing lights from an army of cars lit up the grey skyline, their sirens flooding the air and adding to the ever-growing list of vehicles in pursuit of the rogue hearse.

Behind the vast, three-inch thick windows of the departure lounge, Mr and Mrs Eccles – who had arrived two hours early for their annual holiday to the Isle of Man – were sitting watching the planes refuel on the apron while eating chicken liver pâté sandwiches and salted peanuts. Mrs Eccles dropped her half-eaten sandwich onto her lap and turned to her husband. 'Bernard look, terrorists.'

'More than likely, dear,' replied Bernard before dropping a peanut into his mouth and sucking on it.

'A terrible business.'

'Terrible dear.'

'We shouldn't have to watch this, we're on holiday.'

Bernard nodded in agreement whilst dusting his salty lips with his handkerchief.

Mrs Eccles jerked her head forward suddenly after spotting a crowd of people holding video cameras in front of the parked planes. 'Ooh, is that a news team?'

'More than likely dear.'

'Quickly, get your binoculars out.'

The Essex Regional News Network had the good fortune of finding themselves first at the scene after being sent out to report on another story of an airline going bust. This could be just the scoop the network needed, after being plagued for so

long by funding cuts and low ratings. The team were frantically preparing themselves to go live, although they had little
information on the events unfolding. They had managed to
construct a flimsy-looking gazebo to protect them against the
hail, craftily pinning it down by four suitcases borrowed from
a nearby trolley.

'Right, we need two cameras, as close as you can get on
the vehicles, and one on Clive. You ready mate?'

Clive took a deep breath in and held his thumb up.

'3,2,1 and action.'

The light at the front of the camera switched to green.

'This is the Essex Regional News Network, I'm Clive
Roper, good afternoon. We are broadcasting live from
London's City Airport where there is a dramatic high-speed
car chase taking place across the airport runway. We have
been informed that the serious security breach happened
approximately ten minutes ago when three men in a hearse
forced their way onto the runway at gunpoint. They are now
being pursued by ten airport security vehicles. I must stress at
this point in time we have no reason to believe this is a
terrorist incident. We'll soon be bringing you live footage of
the chase as it unfolds here on London City Airport runway.'

With only a hundred metres between itself and Gary's plane,
the hearse took a sudden jolt forward. Ross looked in his rear-
view mirror to see Lance's contorted face behind his Beamer
windscreen, oscillating between various shades of purple and
screaming unintelligible threats. Lance rammed his foot down
on the acceleration pedal and pulled up level to the hearse.
He opened the window and yelled as loudly as he could, 'Pull
over you fackin' idiot! This is your last chance.'

Ross smiled and flicked up his middle finger as he sped
across a grass verge onto the Centauri Airways landing strip.

Lance pulled down sharply on his steering wheel and slammed into the side of the hearse. It was a body blow that had little impact on Ross but caused Lance to lose control of his steering and career into the path of a luggage trolley, flipping his car in an acrobatic 360-degree spin – it came to land on its side, wheels spinning in torrents of grey smoke.

'They'll be lucky to escape that,' said Mrs Eccles, her binoculars flat up against the departure lounge window. 'If they do they'll be eating their dinner though a straw.'

Bernard dropped a large handful of peanuts into his mouth.

'Exciting, isn't it?'

'Hmmm,' mumbled Bernard, his cheeks bulging like a bloated squirrel.

'Don't eat all the nuts, Bernard, not before flying, you remember what happened last year?'

'Yes dear… sorry.'

Directly below the Eccles, the news team appeared to be cobbling together some basic semblance of order, just in time for Clive to go live with their next update.

'We bring you breaking news. It appears likely that, the pursued passenger from Centauri Airlines Flight C941 is the 1980s pop star Gary Numan. At this point there is only speculation as to why he is being chased and there are far more questions than answers. Is Gary Numan part of an international terrorist cell? Is he wanted for aviation offences? Or could it simply be a publicity stunt prior to the concert he is playing next week at the Royal Albert Hall? These are just some of the questions the bewildered airport staff and passengers are asking themselves as they watch these events unfold.'

The door to the airplane levered open and Gary was the first to step out onto the motorised passenger stairs – he wrapped a scarf tightly around his neck as the hail lashed against him. He sure as shit wasn't in LA anymore. He stopped and looked up to see the flash of sirens careering towards him – and Ross only fifty metres away – and so shouted down to a member of the ground staff on the runway, 'That hearse is heading right for us.' Thinking on his feet, the man jumped into the cab of the passenger stairs and, with Gary teetering above him, quickly reversed and took off down the runway at an impressive top speed of twenty miles-an-hour. Ross, followed by Stubber's green transit van, only just led the chase as the security vehicles closed in more and more by the second. Clinging desperately to the support rails, Gary squinted through the hail to try and get a look at who was at the wheel of the hearse. 'Is that… Ross?'

'I think he's recognised you,' said the Count.

'Take the wheel.' Ross leaned out of his window and fired a shot off at Gary. A deafening crack rang out as the bullet split the air, hitting the steel step beneath Gary's feet; he stumbled forward but managed to grab the railing and steady himself.

'Yeah, well I recognise you too, E.T. isn't it?'

'Huh huh.'

The hearse was now directly behind the passenger stairs. Ross tried to pull alongside the vehicle, but the airport worker was one step ahead. He started to snake from side to side to prevent him getting a clearer line of sight. Ross was growing more and more irate at every turn. The stairs may not have had speed but they did have size on their side.

Next to the Count, the third amigo had, until now, sat in a brooding silence. His gaunt weasel face twisted further with every setback, until his frustration exploded and, sticking his finger in the Count's face, he barked, 'Recargas y disparamos.'

'What's he saying?'

'Why are you asking me?' said Ross.

'I thought you could speak it?'

'I only got an 'O' level.'

'Apuntar a las ruedas.'

The Count raised his voice, 'I don't know what you're saying mate?'

'Las ruedas, la ruedas!'

'I think that means wheels,' said Ross.

'Bastardo inglés.'

'Hey, I bloody well know what that means.'

The Spaniard pulled out his gun, took his seat belt off and joined Ross for the next firing spree. Gunfire rained from the hearse, puncturing the back tyres of their target. The stairs, buckling under the pressure loss, started to sway.

Gary was now lying down on top of his briefcase, gripping the top deck of the runaway stairs. He looked over the edge to see if was possible to drop down on top of the driver's cab. He pulled himself forward to get a better view but inadvertently let his briefcase slip from under him. It cascaded down the steps before splitting open and scattering its contents all over the runway.

Just as the three amigos were reloading, the hearse was rammed from behind. The third amigo was thrown forward, face smashing on the dashboard and slumping unconscious into the footwell. This time it was Stubber's van in the rear-view mirror. 'Have that you blue haired tosser! I told you she wouldn't let us down, didn't I?'

In the back of the hearse, the lid of Granny Bamford's coffin lifted up at the edge. Ever so slightly. Forming a gap just large enough for a small red neon wire to drop out and slither towards the front of the vehicle.

Stubber rammed them again, making Ross drop his gun, which was sent scuttling away along the tarmac.

'Shit, we should have finished them off when we had the chance.'

'That wasn't the directive.'

'Fuck the directive… look where that got us.'

The coffin lid lifted higher, as more neon wires fell to the floor, wriggling forward like demonic eels.

'All the proof I gave them but they never believed me… no one ever does…. is that fair? Is it?'

The Count shook his head slowly as the sweat poured down his face.

'They will soon' – Ross pointed to the gun in the stairwell – 'sometimes there's no choice but to step up.'

The coffin lid crashed down into the back of the hearse as hundreds of glowing wires spilled from the coffin like boiling noodles. Granny Bamford toppled out of the coffin; her putrid face squashed against the side window. Her arms –orches-trated by the wires – smacked against the window like those of a mechanical puppet trying to claw its way out.

'Granny Bamford's been resurrected!' shouted Stubber.

'It's the zombie apocalypse,' said Pete trying to get a picture on his phone, 'I told you it was coming.'

'What's going on back there?' said Ross, taking back the

steering wheel as the Count turned to see what the commotion was all about. 'Er… it's the… um… wires. They're out.'

'Get that fucking lid back on now!' Ross managed to pull alongside the passenger stairs, giving him a better view of the driver and the top platform where Gary was lying, face down, white-knuckled, clinging on. He fired off two more shots, narrowly missing Gary's leg.

'It's too late—' the Count was suddenly dragged down into the footwell on top of his unconscious comrade.

'I need to get a better angle, hold the wheel again.'

'I can't… help!… urghhahhh!'

Ross looked down. The Count was swarming with the little wires, burrowing their way into his ears and eyes, his body writhing in agony. 'Shit!'

Ross could feel the wires crawling up his legs and filling his lap. He tried to beat them off with his gun handle – but there were too many. The wires gave off little sparks as they fused together to wrap themselves around his torso, so tightly he could barely breathe. In a last desperate bid, he stuck his arm out of the window and aimed his gun towards Gary. His index finger quivered on the trigger. He knew this was his last chance. Just as he was about to squeeze, Granny Bamford flew forward and slammed into the window screen. Her arm went through the steering wheel, jerking it downwards, sending the hearse careering off towards the opposite end of the runway. Ross tried to regain control of the vehicle but his strength was fading. He pulled at Granny Bamford as hard as he could but the wires were almost covering his body – drilling into him with their razor-sharp pincers.

The security vehicles were now parallel with Stubber's van, waiting for the right moment to intervene.

'Come on you bastards, what are you waiting for?' screamed Ross as he attempted a last-ditch effort to yank at Granny Bamford who – rather gracefully considering the circumstances – peeled away from the window.

With full vision now restored, Ross had just long enough to read the words 'Aviation Fuel' before ramming into the side of the tanker in front of him.

The force of the explosion nearly knocked Stubber's van clean off its wheels. The flash was blinding. Blue and white flares were shooting through the dark sky, twisting and writhing – as if waging war with the hail that threatened to extinguish their spectacle. Five's tinnitus rang so loud his skull rumbled. They watched as the emergency vehicles methodically arranged themselves around the accident. Stubber and crew slowed to a halt, the flames reflecting on their eyeballs.

On the runway a little way behind the van, a flashing object in the wing mirror caught Stubber's attention. He backed up, opened his door and reached down to scoop it up. It was a small gold box with two buttons embedded into its lid.

'What do you reckon this is?' Stubber passed it into the back of the van. They moved it between themselves in silence. No one could bring themselves to mention the suffocating smell of sulphur and burning flesh. It was all too much for Five, the van had started to spin. Putting pride aside and gathering his courage, he laid his head down on Tina's lap and looked up at her. 'I wish that hadn't happened.'

Tina ran her hands over his back, 'We all do honey… we all do.'

Meanwhile, Clive Roper was back on air for the final broadcast of the day. 'We have now been moved from the runway up to the departure lounge, where hundreds of terrified holiday makers are watching the airport emergency services tackle a dramatic inferno. This is a disaster that has left holiday makers stunned, here at London City Airport today.'

Clive cupped his hand over his ear piece to hear the latest update from head office. '—And we have just received official word from the British Aviation Service that Gary Numan is not wanted for any aviation offences. This just adds to the confusion and intrigue here during these desperately tense moments. With so many questions still left unanswered about the events that have just taken place, we are now going to talk to a Mr and Mrs Eccles who watched these dramatic events unfold from the departure lounge. Can you please tell the viewers how this awful scene affected you?'

'It was dreadful I could hardly bare to watch. I'm 78 I shouldn't have to be subjected to this kind of thing it's not good for my nerves I'm supposed to be going on holiday! We don't even know if our insurance will cover us. Someone said they were religious terrorists, does that mean it's an act of god? I said to my husband it's a terrible business didn't I dear?'

Bernard nodded whilst slipping his binoculars back into his bag. 'Terrible business, dear.'

30

SLIPPERY WHEN WET

15th January

It was 9.15am at the Watt's residence. Don, feeling much more like his old self, was in his bedroom ensconced in a particularly blissful meditation aimed at transcending all notions of the illusory phenomena that is mistakenly referred to as 'the self'. Mags was downstairs on the sofa with one cup of tea, two digestive biscuits and three trashy gossip magazines. Five was in the bathroom arguing with his dad about the last time he had washed his hair. He was certain it was over a month ago but Frank was adamant it was only a week. It was a dispute that found Frank suspended naked on his bath lift, holding a bottle of shower gel in one hand and a tub of beard oil in the other. In order to break this stalemate, Five would need to engage high level diplomacy skills – as complex as any Brexit policy negotiation – though not quite as slippery. The situation was not helped by the repetitive buzz coming from Five's pocket.

'Hello.'

'Five?'

'Yeah?'

'Candice.'

'Alright?'

'You're causing a bit of a stir ain't ya?'

'Huh?'

'Tell 'em to call back later,' said Frank, irritated by the interruption.

'Shut up Dad.'

'I've had Mr Morris on the blower all week,' continued Candice, 'he's been proper bending my ear, he's only trying to get us to change the result of the tournament. I told him, we're not corrupt yeah? We can't just change things coz he's got a bee in his bonnet.'

'Right—'

'He started quoting clauses at me from my own fan clubs, 'Articles of Association.' I said to Lance, that can only mean one thing babe.'

'What?'

'He must have fackin' read them.'

'Right—'

'Do you know how long they are?'

'I once had a—'

'Do you have any idea the pressure Lance has been under with us going into liquidation?'

'I can't imagine.'

'I wouldn't normally share private stuff about my Lance, but he's being treated for erectile dysfunction. It's the stress you see yeah?'

'OK.'

'Anyway, I told Mr Morris I'm not changing nuffin' and I'm not willing to discuss it *any* further.'

'Good for—'

'Do you know what I asked him?'

'No.'

'I said what about *my* reputation? When you've climbed this high on the social ladder you have to fink about these things yeah?'

'I'm sure—'

'At the end of the day it's all about having principles and respect, do you get what I mean babe?'

'Of course—'

'Fat old cunt.'

Five cleared his throat.

'But anyway, I've got some better news, guess who I had on the dog and bone last night?' Said Candice.

'Don't know.'

'You'll never guess.'

'OK.'

'Guess who?'

'Don't know.'

'He just rang out the blue.'

'Who?'

'Only bleedin' Gary Numan!'

'Really?'

'God as my witness!'

'What did he say?'

'It was a bit of blur babe to be honest, I came over all funny.'

'What did he say?'

'I mean what do you say to your all-time hero?'

'What did *he* say?'

'Alright, keep your fackin' wig on.'

'It's not a—'

'He's only requested your band support him when he plays the Royal Albert Hall, he wants you on after the Barry Numans.'

'FUCK!'

'I know babe yeah? You've hit the jackpot!'

'I can't believe it.'

'After I put the phone down on him, I had all this nervous energy yeah? I mean what are you supposed to do after chatting with your all-time idol?'

'I dunno, I can't wait to meet him.'

'I couldn't concentrate for toffee.'

'Right.'

'I couldn't even sit still.'

'Hmm.'

'In the end I had to go upstairs for a wank.'

Five cleared his throat again.

'Don't tell Lance.'

'I won't.'

'By the way Gary lost something at the airport yeah? A small gold box. He wanted me to ask around to see if anyone had found it, he's very eager to get it back.'

'Oh yeah, Stubsy found it on the runway. We'll bring it with us.'

'I'll see you at the gig then yeah?'

'Cheers.'

Frank threw his threadbare towel at Five. 'Who the bloody hell was that? I'm freezing to death 'ere.'

Five picked up the shower head, turned the tap on and sprayed cold water over his dad.

'Ahhh! What are doing you lunatic?!'

Five shouted at the top of his voice, 'We're playing the Royal Albert Hall next week!'

31

BREAK A LEG

21st January

Mags and Don were being treated to a personal tour while the rest of the boys had opted to raid the dressing room mini bar. After all, you could see the Royal Albert Hall anytime. Far better to play actors sat in front of the brightly lit dressing tables that occupied a whole side of the dressing room, which in itself was bigger than most of the venues they normally played. Pete and Five had both slapped on more makeup than an aging geisha girl and now turned their attention to Frank, despite his vehement protests. The last time he'd been forced to wear eyeliner for a photo shoot, he'd forgotten to remove it and got called a bender outside the local church. That vicar had a real mean streak. Five minutes of undignified manhandling was all he could take before, still tired from recent events, he wheeled himself to the other side of the room to hoist his foot up onto the arm of a red velvet chaise longue. A gnarly big toe stuck out from an old brown sock that had been darned more times than it had been washed. He picked up Five's pocket mirror and groaned at his reflection. As he had suspected, black lipstick with a grey frizzy beard is not a great look for a 76 year old man. Who would have known? Make no mistake though, this was how Frank was going on stage. As a result of late-night negotiations – that ended with threats of draconian sanctions – Frank had agreed to the full Numanoid makeover package, which unfortunately included the dreaded thigh-length bondage boot. He sighed deeply and stuffed a handful of cheese and onion crisps down his gullet. There was no way out of it this time: a whole month without hobnobs would be, quite simply, unbearable.

'Right everyone' – Five stood up –'one of the ushers told me that Numan's gonna pop in and say hi before the gig so whatever you do, just… be cool, let me do the talking. Especially you Pete—'

'Charming.' Pete snapped his blusher case shut.

'And you, Dad – in fact all of you just zip it, right?'

'He wants to impress his boyfriend,' said Frank, giving Stubber a wink.

'He's only flesh and blood ain't he?' said Stubber, tightening up his ponytail. 'I'm gonna tell him all about my "metal rhythms" if you know what I mean?' Stubber returned the wink to Frank.

You bastard.

'You just need to chill out.' Pete reached into his clammy army jacket pocket and pulled out a small vial containing little white pills. 'I've got a little something for you.'

Five smiled. 'You taking the piss?'

'Trust me brother, this is legendary medication, it'll jack your performance up to nuclear proportions.'

'Really?' Five flicked his eyes towards the ceiling.

'Straight up, remember Tea-bag Trish from the squat… the homeopath?'

Five nodded, puckering his lips as he exhaled, hard.

'She went to a Pistols gig in '77, it was a blinding set apparently, but here's the thing: halfway through the encore Sid Vicious gobbed the chunkiest phlegm torpedo she'd ever seen across the stage and it landed right in front of her. Luckily she had the foresight to scoop it up and wrap it in an empty crisp packet. When she got back home she used it to create a sacred homeopathic proving which was passed onto me after she died.' Pete stood and held the vial up to a spotlight for maximum effect. 'In this little bottle is the pure, unadulterated and absolute spirit of punk rock, and I've added in a couple of ticklers just for good measure.'

'It's tempting mate, but I'll pass.'

'Think about it for a minute, a normal homeopathic remedy would only have a molecule of saliva for a base, but these little beauties have been brewed from a whole gob full.'

'I'll take one,' said Stubber jumping up from his seat and holding his palm out. 'I'm celebrating tonight, I've just found out that Rambo is going to make a full recovery.'

There was a knock at the door; Five froze in anticipation. *Could it be?* It certainly could. Gary Numan appeared before his eyes, the living embodiment of all that was holy in Five's world. But this was no apparition.

'Is it OK to come in?'

Five, closely resembling Ötzi the Iceman, attempted a response – any sort of noise would have done – but regrettably he encountered a software malfunction, rendering him incapable of speech. *Shit shit shit!*

'I wanted to say thanks for last week,' said Gary, 'I don't think I would have made it through without you guys.'

As Gary crossed the room towards him, reality seemed to blur, like the room had entered warp drive. Five tried to speak again, couldn't and quickly realised it must be only him that was affected. The most important moment of his life to date and he got stuck in a self-imposed panic bardo, in which the only sensation apparent to him was the bead of sweat trickling down his temple.

Pete threw his hand in Gary's direction.

Don't say anything, Pete, please.

'I fucking love your music brother.'

Nooo.

Five felt as if he were locked behind a frosted glass screen. *If I managed to scream, would anyone even hear?* The bead of sweat continued its meandering procession down his neck.

'I've never met a rock star before,' said Stubber, slapping Gary on the back. 'Apart from the Quo backstage at a gig in '74—'

Please Stubsy, don't.

'Nice to meet you, Mr Numan.' Frank wheeled himself over with his right hand whilst brushing a pebble dashing of soggy crisps out of his beard with his left.

Why is this happening?

'Did you know Rick Parfitt was a Woking lad?' Stubber pulled out a chair from one of the dressing tables for Gary to sit down.

It felt like a mini death every time one of them spoke. Five's heart thumped inside his chest like a marching drum; he wasn't sure if speech would be possible but he had to find a way of shutting everyone up. *Let's try again.*

'It's… amazing to meet you… Gary… I'm Five.' His voice squeaked like rusty bicycle brakes.

'And you, thanks so much for your letter, I don't what would have happened without that.'

He actually got it. He probably got all of them!

'I've just had the police over at my hotel. They said that Ross had all the hallmarks of a stalker fan. He had a history of delusional psychosis apparently. They found a fake MI5 badge on him too, he used it to fool two alien fanatics he'd met online into setting up an imaginary task force.' Gary stared at the floor. 'To think I employed him, too.'

'The mind boggles,' said Frank before digging back into his packet of crisps.

'I am sorry about what happened to him, though.'

Five nodded his support for that sentiment and now, having found his voice, he felt the compelling urge to make up for lost time. 'It's always been my dream to support you.'

Noooo! Why did I say that? I sound like an arse licker.

'Well, it certainly doesn't come any better than this place does it?'

He thinks I'm a wanker! I can see it in his eyes.

Stubber, showing no sign of abating, nudged Gary. ''Ere, you know your album *Metal Rhythm?'*

No... Please!

Luckily a sharp beeping noise distracted everyone's attention. It was coming from Five's rucksack. As he knelt down and reached inside, he remembered the gold box Stubber had found on the runway. It had been beeping like this on and off all week. He handed it to Gary. 'Is this yours?'

Gary's eyes widened. 'I'm so pleased you found it! I've been obsessing over this for months.'

'What is it?'

'It's a hi-tech game given to me by a friend. I have to type in a certain series of binary digits to crack the code and get inside. The beeps tell me when I've moved up a level. God knows how many levels there are!' Gary snapped open his briefcase and carefully placed the box inside. 'It contains a very special gift, apparently, I'm determined to find out what it is.'

A second head poked round the door. An official type, expensive suit, dripping with entitlement.

'Can The Bombers be ready to take the stage in twenty minutes, please?'

'Shit,' said Five, 'where's the hair spray?'

Frank, holding the bondage boot up to Gary with a forlorn look on his face, said, ''ere Mr Numan, you couldn't give me an 'and on with this flippin' thing could you? I'm gonna do myself an injury.'

'Don't ask him that, Dad.'

'No, it's fine,' said Gary, 'it's the least I can do.' He bent over towards Frank and, raising his voice, remarked, 'You must be the oldest Numanoid in town.'

'I'm into Fleetwood—'

'It's brave dressing like that at your age,' continued Gary, 'you're an inspiration.'

'That's what I told him,' Stubber joined in with a smirk on his face. 'I mean a lot of people out there might say he looks like a fucking idiot' – Gary nodded in agreement – 'but you definitely can't say he's not making an effort, can you?'

Frank glared across the room as his son grumbled death threats under his breath.

'Come on, then, let's get you ready.' Gary grabbed the boot and pulled Frank's bony leg towards him.

Out in the auditorium the excitement was growing. Over five floors, thousands of Numanoids scoured the aisles to find their allotted red velvet seat. This building was a living masterpiece. Rising up from behind the stage, spear-like pipes spread out from an imposing grand organ. In the glass domed ceiling above, little acoustic discs hovered like an army of flying saucers preparing to land. *I Die You Die* was belting out from the tinsel-draped speakers as the roadies scurried frantically across the stage with their last-minute preparations.

Gary, still grappling with Frank's boot, called over to Five, 'How did you find out about Ross?'

Pete puffed his chest out. 'I think I'd have to take the

credit for that – I hacked his email and found an encrypted file. It was—'

'—a group effort' – Five finished his sentence.

'What did it say?' asked Gary, undoing the boot's buckles to get to the zip.

The room was quiet while everyone waited for someone else to speak. Five decided to take the initiative. 'It was a ludicrous – obviously faked – document, saying—'

'—that you're from another planet' – Pete finished his sentence.

'But it's obviously nonsense,' Five qualified.

Seemingly unfazed by the accusation, Gary appeared more concerned with the problem at hand. He positioned the boot at an angle in front of Frank and slowly tried to guide his leg into it. 'Hmm, interesting… what if I said it wasn't nonsense?'

'So you *are* an alien?!' Pete almost ejected from his seat.

Gary nodded demurely, then turned to Frank, 'Are you sure this is the right size?'

Frank looked back with eyes the size of hubcaps.

'Hallelujah!' howled Pete, throwing his arms in the air. 'Are you a shape-shifting reptilian?'

'Yeah, I'm afraid so, and those little neon wires you saw in the hearse, that's our advanced cyborg circuitry, it burrows into the brain stems of its hosts so we can use them as slaves.' Gary grunted as he pushed the boot down on Frank's leg, 'Don't look so surprised, that's the reason I switched to synth music, as it contains complex binary communication frequencies that act as carrier signals back to the mothership. That's what Ross was trying so hard to block… using *my* synth too. Cheeky – but quite clever really.' Having wrestled Frank's leg into the boot, Gary started grappling with the mammoth side zip. 'These zips are a bugger to get moving.'

The room fell quiet again. Five made a face like a goldfish. A dead one. That's gone a funny colour. He looked around at everyone else in the room; and they stared gormlessly back. *Is this really happening?*

'Why' – Five's voice quivered – 'have you come here, though?'

'We move around the galaxy, enslaving weaker lifeforms, a bit like England thought it was doing until recently on this planet, but on a larger scale. Now Ross is neutralised and we have the signal from the mothership back again, we can get started on earth.'

The room seemed to dim, as if a surreal twilight had set in. The boys were barely breathing. All eyes were glued to Gary for fear of missing a single word. Five reached for the crease of his arm. The first time in over a week.

'So… we're all going to become slaves?'

'Ha ha – I'm messing with you!' Gary prodded Frank in the ribs, who was now shrinking into his wheelchair. 'You lot are way too easy to wind up!'

'Fuck me!' shouted Stubber.

'I knew you were joking,' said Frank pushing himself upright.

Five had no words so chose instead to crumple backwards against the wall.

'But what about the document we found?' said Pete

'There are thousands of fake conspiracy documents online, aren't there?' said Gary.

'Exactly,' said Five, shooting Pete one of his dismissive head movements.

'Why would it be encrypted, though?'

Gary shrugged. 'Dunno, to make it look more authentic? I read somewhere online that Hitler is still alive and living on Mars as a transvestite hermit. I don't think that's true is it?'

'Oh, I believe that one!' said Frank.

Everyone nodded and laughed, mainly out of anxious relief.

'What about the wires then?' Pete persisted, though he now looked utterly brow beaten. 'How come they can move?'

'Probably some kind of remote-control gimmick. Ross was always entering stuff like that into competitions.'

The crowd exploded as the evening officially kicked off with a rousing introduction for the first band. 'Ladies and gentlemen, welcome to the Royal Albert Hall, please put your hands together for the winners of this year's ultimate Battle of the Gary Numan Tribute Bands, The Barry Numans!'

And what an entrance they made. They glided onto the stage (with the aid of six roadies) in a life-sized version of the Telekon toy car, whilst performing an eight-part vocal harmony version of *Cars.* They weren't holding back tonight. They were the all-time greatest Numan tribute act, so why in hell should they? No Numan fan on the planet would ever witness such a finely sculpted homage as this. It was a haunting display of harmonic perfection and vocal artistry. The crowd were so captivated by its brilliance that they forgot to clap.

The repeated zip pulling was proving fruitless, so Gary stuck his foot into the seat of the wheelchair to get some leverage before trying again.

'Ahh, you're trapping my leg hairs,' moaned Frank. Anyone would think he wasn't grateful.

Gary tutted under his breath and beckoned Pete over. 'The bloody zip's stuck.'

'Hey Stubsy, have you got any WD40 in the van?'

'I'm not sure, I'm feeling a bit odd.' Stubber ambled off into the corner to sit down and fiddle with his vaporiser.

'I think it's a two-man job,' said Pete, wrapping his arms around Frank's torso.

'Please take it slowly guys.' Frank gripped the arms of his wheelchair in anticipation.

'Don't worry, you won't feel a thing.' Gary yanked the zip upwards with all his force, managing to get it all the way up but taking most of Frank's leg hair with it.

'Aieeeee!'

As the remainder of Frank's crisps flew through the air, Mags and Don were pushed into the room by ushers. Due to Don's condition and Mags' back taking a turn for the worse, neither of them should have made the journey. But as usual no one could stop them. Five had begged them to at least remain in wheelchairs until the gig started. Mags took one look at her husband's leg and howled with laughter.'

'Tell him,' Frank pointed an accusatory finger at his son, 'he won't let me wear my slipper.'

'I'd have gone with the slipper if I were you,' said Gary.

Frank threw his arms in the air. 'See?'

The head of entitlement poked his head back round the door. 'The Bombers to the stage please.'

'Come on then, everyone' – shouted Five – 'this is the moment we've all been waiting for.'

As Gary was leaving the dressing room, Five ran over to him. 'I'm so sorry about Pete, he's a bit eccentric but he means well.'

'No problem. Good luck tonight. I'm off to plan world domination with my evil sidekick.'

Five laughed and held the door open for him.

What a top bloke.

The rest of The Bombers were now ready and forming a semi-orderly queue behind Five. As they left the dressing room, they bumped into Stubber, who was staring intently at the corridor's spiral wallpaper while trying to suck on his vaporiser, the wrong way around.

'We're on now, Stubsy.'

'The walls are so beautiful.' His eyes bulged from his face like two freshly-baked buns.

'He's tripping his nuts off,' said Frank, somewhat relieved he was no longer in a fit state to take the piss out of him.

'What the hell have you given him?' Five glared at a sheepish-looking Pete.

'Are you gonna be OK, Stubsy?'

'I'm not gay.'

'What are you talking about?'

'I only sucked his knob once. It doesn't make me gay.'

'That's definitely *heading* in the right direction,' said Pete with a Cheshire Cat grin on his face. 'Did you see what I did there?'

'No one cares if you are.'

'I'm scared she's gonna leave me... she spends more time with Jesus than me... it would kill me,' tears ran from Stubber's eyes. Never before had Five witnessed even a glimmer of vulnerability in him. With the rest of the band pushing him forward, however, he was forced to leave him marvelling at the cosmic intricacies of this newly discovered secret realm of wallpaper.

Walking down the corridor to the stage, Don transmitted a rare and much needed spiritual teaching to everyone. 'Focus on your breathing, on the rise and fall of the abdomen and, when the music starts, radiate loving kindness to the audience' – all the ingredients they would need to conjure musical nirvana.

Five flung open the stage door and, without flinching, led The Bombers out into the blinding spotlights. It seemed to take an age to reach the microphone stand. The amps hummed, the guitar lead buzzed and Five's pulse pounded in his ears. As he walked across the stage, he thought of all the amazing artists that had stepped out before him onto these well-trodden boards. A thought that could so easily cripple the most confident of men. As the rest of the band took their positions, Five stared out into the expectant crowd, soaking up the atmosphere. Sensing someone close to him, he turned to see Don with his arms by his side, like a soldier reporting for duty except with a guitar over his shoulder and his familiar smile. 'I've got a confession to make.'

'What now?'

'You know the postcards?'

'Yeaaah?'

'They were from me.'

Five stared at his brother for a few seconds before flinging his head back and roaring with laughter. He guided Don back towards his side of the stage, checked everyone else was ready and then grabbed the microphone.

'Good evening London, we're The Romford Bombers and you… are about to be blown away.'

32

DO NUMANOIDS DREAM OF
REPTILIAN BEEPS?

21st January, 8.30 pm

The ushers flitted up and down the aisles like worker ants while The Bombers served up lashings of rock flavoured dopamine to the frenzied crowd. And, at last, there were no prying eyes backstage. Instead, a glaring red light shone from under the dressing room door at the furthest end of the corridor. Inside, the walls and the ceilings shimmered with neon wires, jostling for the best vantage points. A solitary fly appeared and flickered around the dressing table lights until a fat green tongue unfurled across the room and snatched it, mid-air. Draped across the chaise longue, a ten-foot reptilian beast picked at its dry scaly skin with long thin claws. Its tail flapped restlessly from side to side, as it waited for Brewis to hobble towards it, carefully cradling the little gold box. The box's beeping had now given way to a softer, more looping monotone drone that crackled intermittently. Brewis knelt down in prostration before his reptilian lord. The end of a wriggling neon wire was clearly visible, protruding from the base of his skull.

'Master Numan, we have received word from the mothership.'

Gary's sand-coloured eyes blinked rapidly. 'How long?'

'Ten days, Master.'

'At last.'

'When can we begin?'

'Soon Brewis… very soon; we'll start with the Numanoids.' Gary let out a deep guttural laugh. 'They will be such *easy* pickings.'

'Can we set the crawlers on them, Master, please can we?'

'Yes Brewis…. we'll haunt their very dreams.' Gary looked up at the wires writhing animatedly on the ceiling. 'My beautiful creations… it's time for you to shine.'

A bead of blood popped out of the corner of Brewis's eye and trickled down his cheek. 'We're going to have such fun aren't we master?'

'I think we'll do that rancid little tosser Five first.'

'Can we make him our toilet slave master?' Brewis clapped his hands together in excitement.

'Great idea, Brewis. It was probably those fucking letters that blocked them in the first place.'

Their rapturous laughter echoed down the corridor as the wires slithered down the walls and out of the windows.

Soon they would be in every sewer from London to San Francisco; sharpening their pincers, waiting for the order to attack.

LOVE AND PRIDE

Tina
You guys blew the roof off last night 10:14

Five
Cheers, I loved every second of it! 10:17

Tina
What was it like meeting Gary? 10:19

Five
Amazing, he's a great guy, really funny. He's invited me to join his stage crew for the rest of his tour! 10:25

Tina
Fuck! 10:27

Five
I know, Its a dream come true! 10:29

Tina
I'm proud of you. 10:31

Five

All that alien stuff, total bollocks 10:35

Tina

Yeah, Pete needs help 10:36

Five

Meet up when I get back? 10:38

Tina

I've not blown it then? 10:40

Five

We'll have to see won't we? 10:43

Tina

I'm sorry 10:51

Five

You should be 10:52

Tina

Aye 10:55

Five

You were right about me not taking responsibility though. I've been blaming anyone and their dog for how I've been feeling. I even do it with Romford, there's nothing wrong with this place. It's my home. I love it. 10:56

Tina

Glad to hear it. 10:58

Five

What about you? Still wanting to do something to make your dad proud? 11:01

Tina
I have 11:03

Five
??? 11:05

Tina
I spent 39 years with a wonderful, creative and loving man 11:07

Five
Very good, (but you're gonna have to work so much harder than that) 11:09

Tina
Aye I know 11:10

WHAT NEXT?

You made it to the end. It is my sincere hope that the story made you, at the very least, smile. If you did enjoy the book, it would be amazing if you could leave a review on Amazon for me. The amount of positive reviews the book has effects how visible it is in the online book swamp. Thanks in advance, it really means the world. I'm currently writing the second book in the Alternative 80s series. It's called the Imaginary Man. Any idea who it could be about?

If you would like to see some of the Numan Versus Numan promo video outtakes (Including a tasty interview with Ross) and get some of my books for free.
Join my readers list here:

www.nickyblue.com/reads

You are also welcome to join my Gary Numan Giveaway. As part of my promo push for this book I'm giving away a signed CD (Excile) and a signed Single (Change Your Mind) It closes on February the 15th 2020. Just visit the link below.
Good luck!

https://kingsumo.com/g/l1xnk5/gary-numan-giveaway-one-signed-cd-and-one-signed-single

You can see my other books and audiobooks here

www.nickyblue.com/books

ACKNOWLEDGMENTS

In no particular order. I owe massive thanks to all of the following beings:

Flo: Because she's amazing.

Vicky: Because she is cool.

Simon Murnau: Content editing, proof reading, photos, video, moral filter and brother.

Bobby J: Ideas and sounding board guru. My comedy muse in human form.

Ella Morris: Fantastic artwork

Natalie M Garrett: Proof reading, inspiration and faith.

Chris Callard: Story feedback and cover advice.

Chris Head: Wonderful mentoring.

Richard Gilpin: Videos and Inspiration.

Michelle Cobin: Proof reading, mint tea and encouragement.

Ma and Pa Blue: For encouraging me all the way.

And all my lovely friends for listening to my nonsense.

Beta Readers: Eleanor Dawson, Tracy Hind, Alison Gann, Gurdy Simm, Nathan Mooncie

COPYRIGHT

COPYRIGHT 2019

Numan Versus Numan

First edition.

Copyright © 2019 Nicky Blue

All rights reserved.

Printed in Great Britain
by Amazon

35063090R00170